HOME

Nicola Davies is an author and zoologist. She graduated from Cambridge with a degree in zoology before going on to work in television. *Home*, her first novel for children, was inspired by her own experiences growing up. "I wanted to write something adventurous and exciting that was also about where human beings fit in the world – something I know I thought a lot about when I was growing up. All young people search for their identity, and it can be a painful and confusing process; what helped me was finding a relationship with nature, with the landscapes around my home in Suffolk. So in *Home*, Sacks and Nero are finding out who they are and in doing so are finding that they are part of earth and have a kinship with all living things." Nicola is also the author of the non-fiction books *Poo, Big Blue Whale, Surprising Sharks* and *Ice Bear*.

D0063486

For Joseph and Gabriel,
and for Katie S who heard it first

This is a work of fiction. Names, characters, places and incidents are either
the product of the author's imagination or, if real, are used fictitiously.

First published 2005 by Walker Books Ltd
87 Vauxhall Walk, London SE11 5HJ

2 4 6 8 10 9 7 5 3 1

Text © 2005 Nicola Davies

The right of Nicola Davies to be identified as the author of this work has been
asserted by her in accordance with the Copyright, Designs and Patents Act 1988

This book has been typeset in Frutiger Light

"The Flower-fed Buffaloes" by Vachel Lindsay is reprinted with the permission
of Nicholas C. Lindsay on behalf of the Estate of Vachel Lindsay.

Printed and bound in Great Britain by J. H. Haynes & Co. Ltd

British Library Cataloguing in Publication Data:
a catalogue record for this book is available from the British Library

ISBN 0-7445-5983-9

www.walkerbooks.co.uk

HOME

NICOLA DAVIES

WALKER BOOKS

AND SUBSIDIARIES

LONDON · BOSTON · SYDNEY · AUCKLAND

The flower-fed buffaloes of the spring,
In the days of long ago,
Ranged where the locomotives sing
And the prairie flowers lie low;
The tossing, blooming, perfumed grass
Is swept away by wheat,
Wheels and wheels and wheels spin by
In the spring that still is sweet.
But the flower-fed buffaloes of the spring
Left us long ago.
They gore no more, they bellow no more,
They trundle round the hills no more,
With the Blackfeet lying low,
With the Pawnees lying low.

"The Flower-Fed Buffaloes" by Vachel Lindsay

prologue

3 August 2067

The Manhattan Announcer

Supa Group to Save Lives

A group of powerful businessmen nicknamed the Supas met at a secret location in Manhattan today to discuss the growing environmental crisis. It was a meeting that will decide the fate of the millions of Americans who have so far survived the effects of catastrophic environmental pollution.

The group, composed of leaders of the biggest companies in the country, is the only organization with the resources to stop the mounting death toll from widespread starvation and poisoning. Seventy per cent of the eastern seaboard's water sources are now officially designated as toxic and reserves of grain and other food sources are running low. With the continuing drought in the grain belt, following the acidification of soil, there is little prospect of a change in this situation.

Spokesman for the Supas Darrell Nabisco said in a preliminary statement, "We have to face the fact that it is no longer possible for any form of life to survive outside the protection of a building. Over the next two years the Supa companies will undertake a building programme to protect major cities from the effects of toxic rain and smog. We will also provide indoor food-producing facilities and safe accommodation for crop workers outside the cities. We have to face the fact that the number of workers that can be accommodated in these facilities is extremely limited." Mr Nabisco added, "To safeguard security of food supplies, it will be necessary for workers in these new facilities to agree to a strict code of conduct..."

sacks

HUMANS didn't belong on Earth, that's what TV always said. We'd come from somewhere else – from Planet Home. That's why things on Earth were toxic and alien. Inside our buildings was the only place we were safe.

So the first time I lay down Outside, on the Earth, I was afraid. I shut my lips tight so that the spiky green stuff Mott called "grass" wouldn't poke in. I closed my eyes too. I didn't want the rain getting in. But the wetness was in my face and the smell of the Earth filled my head up. I didn't like like it. *I don't belong here,* I thought. *No one does.*

Mott had me pressed flat, belly down, so it was hard to talk without letting grass and water into my mouth. But I managed it anyway because I was so angry with him.

"Wanna go back!" I hissed, "I *am* goin' back!" But Mott's old fingers were like metal, his arm like a machine clamping on my spine, holding me still.

"Shuddup, Sacks," he said.

So I shut up and thought how soon I'd be big enough to stop doing what Mott said. He was a freak to come Outside all the time, not caring about getting poisoned. *You're a freak Mott*, I told him in my head.

The wet cold of the ground began to spread up through me. I kept it back with thoughts of Station 27, where we lived, warm and dry under the big dome roof. Everything there was always comfortable and safe. No wind, no rain or cold, or anything toxic. And never a thing you didn't expect. All days there, inside, had the same pattern. In the mornings Mott and I worked on the weed tanks. The weed was grown for food. Every month we cut it all and put it in a big masher so it could be taken away and made into stuff fit to eat. I liked that part of the day, plunging my arms into the warm water, full of blue lights, and stroking the silky green strands. I even liked the way the water left a salty taste on my arms when it dried, a little crust to scratch off.

But I didn't like the afternoons, when we checked the Unit sheds. Units made my skin crawl, and there were hundreds of them in the sheds. They sat on shelves, row upon row of them; pink wrinkly blobs, the size of your head. They weren't really alive, or so we were always told, but they flinched when you touched them and their little wet input holes sucked at the pipes, like mouths. But Units were important, or at least what came out of them was important: a kind of clear goo with yellow blobs in, called "Product", that our bosses, the Supas, set great store by. Every bit of Product coming from the Units' output tubes had to be weighed and measured before the Supas took it away in tanks, along with the weed, in their big aero-crafts. If any Product went astray, there was trouble.

TV said that Units were from Planet Home and had been brought all the way to Earth to make Product for us Workers. It was a special kind of food to help keep us strong. All the same, I didn't like Units. They were smelly, and I hated having to push pipes back into their nasty gooey little openings. I didn't mind it so much when I was small, because of Mott; him teaching me how to do the work; making me laugh and telling tales of how the Station was years ago. But Mott didn't make me laugh any more. Nothing seemed to please him, and all he thought about now was his trips Outside. So it was all fight and bad feeling between us, and there were no jokes and stories to help take away the sadness and the stink in the Unit sheds.

The cold had got right through from my belly to my back now, but still Mott held me. "You awake?" His voice was in my ear, raspy and whispering.

"Course I'm awake. 'Tis too cold 'ere for dozing!"

"Hush then," he said. "They're coming! Look!" And now Mott's voice was soft; kind, like it hadn't been in a long time. So I forgot how angry I was with him for bringing me Outside, and I lifted my face out of the wet grass to look.

We were a long way from the Station. Much further than I'd thought. All the way out I'd looked at my boots and cursed

Mott, not thinking of the distance. Now the Station was just a grey shape, so small, and all around it was the Outside, big and empty. Outside went everywhere, in every direction, flat and green, with the grey sky over it. There was patch of dirty brown water stretching before us in the green. But I knew Mott wasn't interested in any of that. I saw right away what he wanted me to look at: two white shapes coming through the air towards us. Closer and closer they came. It was wings that moved them, but not wings like on human aero-craft. These wings moved up and down, slow, struggling through the air like it was thick .

Aliens, that's what they were. Creatures that *belonged* here on Earth, where humans never did. I was so, so frightened. All my life I'd heard TV say that there were still Aliens Outside, and Aliens were dangerous. They could attack you, kill you straight off, or just give you some disease that'd finish you. I wanted to get up and run, but old Mott fired up was really strong. I was pinned, flat as a nail head, while the white beings flew on. They got so close, so big, they were all I could see; and the whoosh of their wings was all I could hear. I was sure it was my last moment. I was going to be killed by Aliens, just like TV always said you could be. I shut my eyes again. I would have screamed, but I had no breath.

And then... Nothing. A splash. Another splash. All quiet. The wind blowing over my ears and Mott's wheezy breathing. I slowly opened my eyes, just a crack, enough to look out.

There, beside the muddy patch of water, they had landed. Their long wings had disappeared somewhere, and their shape was smooth again. They looked whiter somehow, like a light bulb growing brighter when the power comes up. Their bodies were streamlined, *perfect* – better than anything we humans could make, I thought – but too big for the legs. Those were as thin as wire and looked ready to snap. Even in my fear I was wondering about them, wanting to know how they were made, how they flew like that, so strangely.

At one end their bodies had a long tube, or arm, that ended in a dark point. The tube waved, bent and twisted. Then I saw that the "tube" was a neck with a small head on the tip. The "point" was a mouth-thing that stuck out, and there were two dark shiny eyes. I was frightened again when I saw those. I'd been seen by an Alien! That made me want to run all over again.

Mott breathed words into my ear. "They're *birds*," he said. "That's what they called, birds."

He didn't need to speak so low, I thought. They didn't care about me and Mott, lying in the grass; we didn't seem to "be" for them at all. They coiled and uncoiled their necks, over their bodies and then up into the air. They ruffled their strange skin, so that one moment it was broken into fragments and the next, whole and smooth again.

I watched them ignoring us, and I stopped being frightened. I felt odd. My heart beat in my throat and I was hot, and then cold. I couldn't take my eyes off the two long-necked white "birds", and I didn't notice the grass spiking, or the rain falling any more.

The birds were making noises at each other. I didn't have words for those sounds then, and I don't now. I could say they screeched like brakes or creaked like hinges. I could say they shouted out like a person saying "Hey!" across a big room, or that they cried like a person with a hurt. But none of that would be right. They weren't human and they weren't machine, so I'd never heard anything like them before. They threw their heads around and opened their pointed mouths to make more and more sounds. At first they took turns, and then they did it together. Louder and louder, faster and faster; joyful seeming; full of life, as I'd never seen anything so full before. Their wings unfolded from wherever they'd been, and they stepped about on their spindly legs. And the thought rose in me like a bright bubble bursting to the top of a tank: *They're speaking*, I thought. *Speaking to each other!* But the weird part was that I felt it was a language I *knew*. Almost like I'd just forgotten it, and in a minute I'd remember it again and understand what they were saying.

I'd never felt such as I felt then, looking at those dancing, talking beings, so beautiful and alive, and *belonging* there in the flat green of Outside. I thought my blood would pop out of my fingertips, that my head would open to the wide sky. I was smiling and crying, and the wind and rain blowing into my open mouth tasted too fresh and sweet to be bad!

The bird on the left was hit first. A great stain of red sprang onto its smooth whiteness from where the blade had stuck. The colour shook me. It was the red of my own blood. How could Aliens have the same blood as us humans from Planet Home, far away in the sky? But it seemed they did. There was no mistaking something so familiar, and showing so brightly there, against the white breast.

The bird fell, its legs bending and its coiling neck arching slowly away from the body. It seemed like a long time before the head hit the water and made the surface crease and wobble. I turned, and there was Mott half standing, with a second blade in his hand, his arm bent ready for another throw. The live bird just stood, tilting its head to look at its friend with one dark eye and then the other.

I was on Mott in one move. Up, jump, kick. The blade went flying into the green. I began to yell, and ran to where the last white bird still stood, amazed. I was almost close enough to touch it when it got the message, and began to run away. But now it didn't look so good, so well made. It was all flop and mess. It staggered into a run, high-stepping along the edge of the water, wings spreading as it went. I was afraid that Mott had somehow thrown another blade and hit it, and broken something inside. Then its legs and wings took on the same beat – one-two, one-two – and it was in the air and getting away from Mott, and from his killing blade.

I stopped running and watched the bird working its wings

up and down, scooping itself up into the sky. I watched until it was gone into the grey distance and I was left behind. I looked down to where the bird had taken off and saw that a tiny shaving of its skin was floating on the water. It was pale and curved, soft as hair. I scooped it up and tucked it inside my clothes.

Mott grabbed my shoulder and spun me round to yell in my face. "Could've got both of they! Both!"

He shook me hard, but I didn't bend my face away like usual. I was flamed up with anger like I'd never felt. I looked into Mott's little eyes in a dip of wrinkles, and shouted right into his face. "Why d'you kill it? The one good thing in all this cold Outside and you killed it! I hate you, Mott."

I threw his hands off me and walked away. He didn't try and follow but just stood at the pond's edge, like the white bird when its friend had fallen, and shouted, "Get findin' that blade."

Of course, I didn't need to be told *that*. Only Supas were meant to have weapons – guns, blades and such. They said Workers like us were too stupid to use 'em right. Not like the clever Supas. Mott said it was nothing to do with cleverness and all to do with fear. Supas were afraid: feared that Workers would turn weapons on them that were always telling us what to do. I wasn't sure if he was right or not, but I knew blades were precious and that Mott would pay me back hard if I didn't find his. So I began to search, and as I did I thought of what TV said about Outside: the deadly Aliens; the poisoned ground that oozed invisible toxins; the pockets of air and showers of rain that could get inside your body and kill you slowly. Mott said that was all lies, but I'd never believed him; seemed quite right to me that a planet where humans weren't meant to be should be poisonous. But now, scrabbling for the blade in the wet grass, I thought, *I've been out here for hours and I've seen Aliens, and none of it's killed me. Leastways not yet.*

I didn't look at Mott while I searched. I didn't want to see what he was doing with the dead bird. I looked up once and saw him bent over its body, pulling wisps of whiteness from its skin in handfuls. They caught in the wind and blew off over the green in sad little trails. I didn't want to think of Mott taking the bird to bits, so I stood away and looked hard in the grass.

I'd kicked the blade a very long way. Strong legs, you see. By the time I found it, it was late and hunger was reaching up from my belly to grab my brains. Much more than hunger it was. The hunger for Station food – Meal One and Meal Two we called them – was like a sickness. If you missed your Meal time, the longing for it came and took you over, until all you felt was the need to get that food, that little foil package of pap.

Thick shadow had gathered at the edges of Outside, but Mott was still messing with the dead bird and wasn't ready to go back. I'd have to go alone. I'd never walked alone Outside in the dark and I was afraid. TV said Aliens moved about more at night. Then I thought of the birds, who were Aliens but seemed no danger to anyone. I yelled to Mott, waving the blade for him to see, and set off. I kept the Station lights in my eye, to guide me, and at every step the hunger got worse. When I thought of what TV said – Meals! You're never hungry with Meals! – I whimpered to myself.

Mott caught up with me just outside the Station walls, and I was so hungry that I didn't notice him till he clamped my arm in his hand. My whole body was screaming now so I didn't care if he shouted, just as long as I could go inside and get my Meal. But he didn't shout. Instead he raised a bag, weighted with the dead bird, and said, "You got to see."

"No! Meal, Meal now!" I tried to pull from him, but I was weak.

"Yes. You got to, Sacks," he said. "So you know to do the same when you need it. So you can live Outside."

I didn't understand why Mott wanted me to be able to live Outside, when all I needed was in the Station. And I didn't want to see what he'd made of that beautiful white bird. So I just shut my eyes and wouldn't look. Mott kept on. "I'll hold you," he threatened, "I'll hold you 'ere all night."

I knew Mott could wait for Meals – he didn't get desperate the way I did. But all I could think of was the food on my tongue, the hit of it in my blood, so I gave in to him.

"All right," I said, "I'll look."

Mott shook the bag upside down, until something slithered out onto the ground. It wasn't at all like the body of the bird: there was no long neck, no wiry legs, no sleek whiteness. Just a pinkish shape smeared with blood.

"They got blood like ours, Sacks," Mott said. "Blood just like ours."

"I know. I saw when you killed it."

"You gotta kill things Outside to stay alive."

"Where's the white?"

"That's feathers," said Mott, excited. "Feathers they're called. Pulled 'em off. You saw." Yes, those wisps in the wind, the little shaving I'd saved inside my jacket. "And the neck too and the legs. You got to cut all them off. Then you puts it on a *fire* and eats the body."

Mott was always having fires. I'd seen the smoke through the portholes of the Station and thought how one day the Supas would see his smoke and catch him at it. And I'd seen fire on the TV, so I knew what it did. I could imagine the bird's body spitting and crackling. It made me feel sick.

"It keeps you alive. Better than Meals, much better." Mott loosed his grip on my arm and spoke softly again. He looked into my face, the way he had when I was small and he had stuff to teach me. "I can show you, Sacks, if you'd let me."

But the thought of the white bird being made into this bloody lump made me shudder, and all I wanted was my Meal. "No. I don't want to know."

"I'll give you some of this bird to eat?"

"No! I want my *Meal*!"

Mott put the pinkish shape back in the bag. "All right. But remember, you'll eat this one day," he said. Then he let me go, without shouting. He seemed sad, not angry at all.

Inside the Station I felt a bit better. I walked to the food store, where the cardboard boxes of Meals were stacked up. I looked up at the big lighted dome of the roof and down at the dry tiles under my feet, and made myself breathe slowly. *Safe*, I thought. *Safe!* But in my hunger I'd forgotten the supply aero-craft. It was late. Tanks of weed and Product were stacked up too high and almost all the Meals were used. I'd have to search hard to find one.

I pressed my palm onto the black-hand symbol on the lid of the first box I came to, triggering it to tell me what was inside. "Meal Two. Empty," said the little electronic voice. I put my hand on the symbol of another box, then another and another. "Meal Two. Empty," said the machine voice over and over. I ran up and down the rows, slapping hands now, my heart beating louder all the time. "Meal Two. Empty." Had I checked this row before? This was bad. I was shaking and sweating, and thinking was harder than ever.

I tried the next row. The first box had a broken lid, and when I put my hand on the symbol it said nothing. I wiped my palm to take away the sweat, and tried again. This time the broken lid popped open and a foil envelope dropped out. A Meal! A Meal Two! I shook it and it began to heat up. I sucked on the fat straw and shut my eyes as the hot paste squirted into my mouth.

But no, I couldn't eat it in the store room. I'd fall asleep there after, and if the delivery aero-craft came in the night, I wouldn't hear the alarm call to help Mott unload. Then I'd be in trouble! I made myself spit out the straw and hurry from the storeroom. *Hang on, hang on just another minute 'til you get to your platform*, I told myself.

Years ago, Mott had always told me, more than a hundred people had lived on Station 27. There'd been sleeping places for them all, leisure rooms, halls to take Meals in company, and a huge swimming pool. Good fights, too, he said – blade fights, with blood spilled. There was plenty of work, with a hundred weed tanks and fifty sheds of Units. But when I came, all that was long gone. Station 27 had one Unit shed and two long tanks. It needed just two people to run it, and two people didn't need sleep spaces and leisure rooms and halls. Just Meals and TV. So Mott and I kept to one end of the Station, near our work, in the last Unit sheds and tank room, and close to the food store. The door to the old part of the Station was welded shut, and beyond it the leisure rooms, halls and the pool were just one big pile of rubble.

With only two of us on Station, and few spare parts being delivered, Mott had to mend everything that broke, and every time he did, he made me do it with him. I'd learned plumbing, electrics, welding – everything. So when Mott began his going Outside, and I stopped liking him, I built my own space. It was far enough from Mott's sleeping place to feel separate, but close to his secret door to Outside, because I still liked to know when he was inside and when he wasn't. I made a platform, tucked under the roof twenty metres above floor level, out of old scaffolding poles and all sorts of things left around the Station. First, I'd used a forklift truck to move an elevator Unit from a disused storeroom, so I didn't have to carry stuff up ladders. Then I'd plumbed in a shower and toilet Unit that I'd found still in its carton. I'd welded metal railings all round and made a metal box bed filled with old packaging for a mattress. The easiest thing had been TV. You could put one anywhere and it would work – didn't need a plug or anything. "You're never alone with TV!" so TV always said.

The moment I was in my elevator, I sucked hard on the straw. Savoury mush came into my mouth and the shouting inside me quieted down. I put my hand in the slot on the control panel and told the lift "up" and it rose, smooth as water. I stepped out into my place and kicked off my boots. I walked about, sucking on my Meal, and the room came alive. Lamps lit up, TV came on and began to chatter. I had filled my sleeping place with colours – bits I'd found left from when the Station was full of people. Orange and blue carpets, a red cover on the bed and yellow bulbs in the lights.

I flopped on the bed and sucked the last from the Meal – a few mouthfuls of sweet mush to follow the savoury – and stared at TV. It was the News. The screen showed pictures of the City where the Supas lived, all bright and gleaming with huge buildings under a great sparkly dome that kept out all the Alien toxicness of Earth. Then there was a picture of a red-haired kid with the pale fat face that all Supas seemed to have. He was dressed in shiny red. TV's voice spoke over the pictures. It was a machine voice but, because I'd known it all my life, it seemed friendly enough.

"Today," it said, "young Fulton Murdoch takes over the leadership of the Murdoch family." That was him, in the red suit. "He appeared at the broadcast tower in the colourful suit once traditional in the Murdoch family." All the other Supa families – the Fords and Ryans, Nabiscos and Chryslers – always wore the same black uniform, Supa blacks. They all had the same colour skin too, pinky white. Not like Workers. We were all colours – blue-black to pale yellow and all shades between – though most of us were brownish, like Mott, and a bit paler than me. Supas were all the same apart from their hair, but that was often slicked down so flat that you couldn't tell what colour it was. They were on TV all the time. Or at least they used to be. Nowadays it seemed like we heard about Murdochs more than anyone else. Still, TV told us, like it always had, that Supa families worked together for all our futures!

TV said that Workers didn't need families. We never had fathers or mothers or brothers or sisters, like the Supas did. TV said Workers were best being "flexible". So we were taken to our first Stations at four years old, and raised through working from the start. No Worker ever knew where they'd been born, nor remembered about their life before Stations. When

Mott was young he was moved around, never in the same place for more than a year. But I'd been on Station 27 all my life. Mott told me he'd fixed that. It was "special" treatment, he said. I'd been glad of it when I was small, but sometimes now I wished I could get a taste of something new.

There was another picture on the screen: Fulton shaking hands with Scurro Nabisco, the leader of the Nabisco family. That was who owned our Station and all the weed and Product Stations. Nabisco's own son came to deliver Meals and take away what we made from the Unit sheds and the tanks. I'd seen this Scurro before. He always looked greyer than the rest of them ever did, with a face that reminded me of a metal slab. "Family leaders work together to defeat our enemies..." TV said as Nabisco and Murdoch patted each other on the back.

"Enemies" meant *Rebels*. Workers who ran away from their Stations and blew things up and shot people. The thought of Rebels made me afraid, though Mott was always saying how they were "giving the Supas what was coming to 'em". Sometimes TV showed close-up pictures of dead Rebels, laid out with blood on their bodies and bullet holes in their heads. Not tonight, though. Tonight my favourite programme followed the News.

It was the same programme that TV showed every night at this time, about life on Planet Home. Home was far away in the stars. It was where humans came from, where we really belonged. Where we would all go back to one day, or so TV said. Nothing on Home was toxic because it was where humans were *meant* to be. Outside on Home was *safe*. TV showed pictures of it: huge tall plants, called trees, that *never* grew on Earth, stretching for miles and covered with fruit you could eat, just like that. On Home, water didn't fall from the sky in toxic rain, or slosh round the land in grey, oily seas; water there was blue and clear, kept in wide oceans that were full of living beings, silver and quick. People lived in cities by the oceans, better even than the City under the dome, where Supas lived on Earth. There were no Stations with weed tanks and Units to make food, because food on Home just *grew* out of the ground. TV showed tall buildings, shiny-bright, reaching up into the blue sky, with people looking out of their windows. The people smiled as they looked out over the blue ocean and sat watching the stars come out in the night sky.

Now it was coming to the part I liked the best. TV zoomed in on one of those stars above the shining skyscrapers, and then on a small, muddy-coloured planet. "This is where you are now. A planet called Earth, far from Home. But your rulers, the Supa families, are working hard in the City, so one day everyone can go Home." The planets faded and a great pointed machine, with long silvery sides, filled the picture. After a moment the machine began to shake, then it began to move upwards into the blue sky. "Millions of us have gone Home already, in rockets like these," TV went on. "We must all keep working hard so that more rocket ships can be built to take everyone Home."

I really liked this programme. Every night I watched it, as my Meal sat in my belly doing its work. I'd fall asleep in front of it and dream of Home, the place where I really, really *belonged*. But tonight my Meal was late, and it hadn't yet made me sleepy and dull. I looked at TV and questions came to my mind. If Home was so good, why had humans left and come to Earth? What exactly were the Supas *doing* to help us get Home? All we ever saw of them was their uniforms and their guns, as they told us what to do and when.

I didn't want to think these thoughts. I didn't want to think *any* thoughts at all. Thinking thoughts was so hard, it almost hurt. So I just I got angry instead, and told TV to "be quiet" and the lights to "go off". And after four tellings. they did.

I lay on my back in the dark and looked up. The station roof was made of thick, misted glass, to let the daylight in. Up close, though, you could see out, just enough to see the stars as blurry points of light in the black sky. I liked looking at stars. I didn't know which one was Home – TV never said – so I just picked one. I saw myself melting through the roof and going straight there, flying in cold space, on my own with nothing but my body. Home would be hanging next to my star, like a drop of water, and I'd float down onto it.

At last, my Meal began to work on me. I felt warm and sleepy. I didn't want to think any more and the nasty questions dropped from my mind. I fell asleep and began to dream.

But I didn't dream of Home. Instead Mott sprang up in my sleeping head. He was holding the white Alien, the bird, tightly in his arms. This time I understood its strange language. "No! No! Help me! Help me!" it yelled in its high voice. I ran and ran, but I couldn't get there before Mott opened his mouth and bit into its feathers!

I sat up fast, wide awake. My movement triggered the lights and TV, and the empty Meal pack fell onto the floor. My head hurt and my clothes were sticky, so I took them off. Tucked inside my top, I found the little white feather from the Alien bird. It had a tiny stalk that I turned between my fingers. It didn't look toxic. Or feel toxic. I stroked my face with the edge of it. "Feather!" I said the word out loud.

I told TV and lights "off!" again, put the feather under my head and fell back asleep and dreamed. There was no Mott this time, or Home, but a dream I'd never had before: a woman stroking my face with a white feather. So I *felt* I was back on Home, even though it couldn't have been true because, in the dream, I *knew* I was still on Earth.

"Unit delivery. Workstation immediately! Unit delivery. Workstation immediately!" The alarm shouted from TV's screen. It must have been going a while, because it stopped pretty soon and TV began the Meal One jingle: "Meal One! Gets your day's work done!"

I got dressed, got in the lift and left TV still singing, "Meal

One! Gets your day's work done!" over and over to pictures of smiling Workers in their bright, baggy overalls, all sucking on foil pouches. No one needed to be told about Meal One or Two. Your body did that for you. Every morning you woke up wanting that fat straw in your mouth, and until you got it, you felt very bad. I went to the food store and found the last carton of Meal Ones pretty quickly. That was a good start! Today would be better than yesterday! With the first suck, the energy came *zing!* into my legs, *buzz!* into my brain. I ran through all four gates between my place and the inner doors of the hangar.

Mott was already there. He didn't tell me I was late. He didn't say anything. He looked out through the porthole in the wall and scowled. Outside, the sky was just getting light, so you could tell the flat, dark ground from the air. The delivery aero-craft showed against the sky. It was coming in low and slowly, with no lights, so when it dropped towards the runway, it disappeared against the black earth. Only the runway lights, stuttering awake, told you it was on its way.

"Why they flyin' dark?" I asked Mott.

"They're taking care," he said. "I reckon they're worried. Feared up. Feared *right* up." He cussed under his breath and mumbled, "They been tipped off. They know something, they do."

I didn't know what he was talking about and didn't want to. These days he was always making out something was up, showing that *he* knew what *I* didn't. "What have they got to be feared of?" I asked. "They're delivering, is all."

"That's all you know!" Mott snapped. "Seems you don't want to know *nothing*, though it's more than time you did!" He turned from the porthole and took me by the shoulders. "They're being cautious 'cos out there, Outside, in what they *calls* 'toxic' is Rebels, Workers that are *free* of Supas and their wicked ways. The Supas' world is coming to an end, Sacks. So you better mind what you seen me do with that bird – you'll need that knowledge soon enough!"

Mott was shouting now, but I didn't care, just yelled right back at him. "You're a freak, Mott. If the Supas' rule is ending then I'm not staying here and I'm not killing Aliens either. *I'm* goin' *Home*."

Mott's face glowed angry and his fingers bit my arms. I thought he might shake me to pieces, but instead he let me go and spoke quietly. "Well, you *might* be going Home. Real Home too. So get covered up, like usual. I ain't hidden you all these years to lose you now."

I didn't know what he meant about keeping me hidden, but that quiet voice made me feel afraid. So, without a word more, I put on the hooded overall that I wore for the Supas' visits.

"You do exactly what I tell you today, right?" said Mott. I nodded and let him pull the hood down over my head.

At the last moment the aero-craft had put on its lights. It landed on the runway and then taxied towards us. I saw it was half the size of our usual craft, a huge, heavy carrier called the

Mandraya. It was smooth and grey, with wings swept back from its sides and three wheels, like black legs, underneath. I guessed it went a lot faster than the *Mandraya*, but would hold far fewer tanks and Meal cartons. I wondered why the Supas had decided to use it. *The* Mandraya *must have engine trouble*, I reckoned.

I pressed my face to the porthole in the door to the hangar and watched the craft come inside. The hangar's metal walls shivered as the engines roared. Its whole body was inside now, and the pilot's voice, flat and dead like all Supas' voices, came crackling over the old speakers. At least it was our regular pilot, Fortay Nabisco, son of the famous Scurro. So in spite of Mott going on, and the unfamiliar craft, things *were* normal.

"Close the outer doors," Fortay told Mott.

Outer doors had to be made secure before the inner doors, into the Station, could be opened. Supas had become especially nervous about that, since there'd been so much talk about "enemies" on TV. I got ready to open the inners, smiling at the thought of all the Meals there'd be on board. But Mott was doing nothing.

"Mott, Mott, close the outers!" I shouted to him but he just stood there, limp. The lights in the hangar began to flicker then went out. Fortay wouldn't like that one bit. I opened the control panel to check their circuit, but Mott yelled at me to stop.

Then Fortay's voice came through the speaker again, sharper and tighter. "Make good the outers!"

I looked at Mott. He stood by the controls like a burnt-out wire, staring at where the Outside showed through the open outer doors. "Mott. Close 'em. He said close 'em!"

"Make good the doors now or we will abort this delivery," warned Fortay.

Abort the delivery! This fast aero-craft could almost turn round in the hangar and accelerate straight out! Inside five seconds it could be gone! I thought of the empty Meal cartons in the food store and screamed at Mott, "Close the doors!" Mott didn't do anything but fold up his eyes and look out past the plane.

"We will abort in ten, nine, eight..." The engines began to drone louder as Fortay prepared to pilot the craft back out.

"Mott!"

"Six, five..."

Mott stopped staring, as if someone had flicked a switch. "Closing doors, Nabisco-sir," he said. "Sorry, Nabisco-sir. Malfunction down 'ere. I'll fix it for next time, eh? Hangar lights back. Circuit malfunction."

What was he on about? I hadn't even looked at the circuit!

"Just get the doors closed, Mott. *Now!*"

The voice sounded so loud that I looked up to where the pale-blue light shone in the bubble of the cockpit. There was Fortay, tall and broad and pale, like his father, only sort of pumped up and brighter coloured. He stood at the window, but he wasn't driving. There was a small figure in the pilot's chair, too small to be a grown-up; Supas started their jobs early in life, just as we did, so that wasn't a surprise. What made me look hard was the pilot's looks: not like other Supas, but dark-skinned and black-haired, like me.

The craft's doors opened and the big ramp pushed out like a stiff tongue, so the Supa and his men could get out. For the last two years, since there'd been so much talk of Rebels on TV, Fortay had taken to bringing two guards with him. One stayed on board, while Fortay and the other guard looked over the loading of Product and weed. But today he and his guards didn't move off the ramp. All three were cov-ered in black body armour, with full helmets and carrying an extra gun apiece. Their weapons showed red lights, so were ready to fire, and the men looked afraid and expecting trou-ble. Mott cussed again when he saw them, then kicked me hard when he saw me staring and made me look down at my boots.

Fortay stood on the end of the ramp, as if the Station was toxic, like Outside. "What was the malfunction?" he asked, his words as fast as bullets.

Mott answered, but he spoke extra slowly and carefully, dragging his explanation out somehow. I got the feeling that something was happening, behind and between things, where I couldn't see it. "Well, Nabisco-sir, the hydraulics on them doors is getting on a bit now. They just—"

Fortay cut him off. "Next time I'll abort," he snapped. "Clear?"

Mott nodded without looking up.

"Get on with loading tanks and unloading new Units. And make it *fast*," ordered Fortay. "Any problem and I'll leave without unloading the Meal cartons. And this isn't the *Mandraya*, remember! This is our fastest craft, the *Uccello*. She can rocket through those doors even if that *malfunction* fails to open them." He turned round and marched back through the *Uccello*'s doors, leaving the two guards standing, fierce-looking, on the ramp.

It was odd and I didn't like it. But at least with Fortay aboard his craft, he couldn't check the Product and weed tanks. If there wasn't enough Product, he couldn't moan about it!

"Right!" said Mott. "He wants it done fast, so we'll do it fast. I'll load the new Units on the ramp and get the tanks sorted. You go down the shed and connect up the new Units as they come."

It wasn't normal to do things like this, but I liked the idea of putting in the new Units on my own, without Mott grumbling down my neck. I turned to go, but Mott grabbed me and hissed into my ear. "You stay there in that shed until I say. You hear?" I nodded, and ran off to get to work.

Inside the shed I flicked on the lights and there were the Units, hundreds of them, stacked four-deep up and down the building, with pipes snaking in at one end of them and out at the other. They didn't make a sound. In fact, it was so quiet in the sheds that I always had to say something to make sure my ears were still working.

"You stink!" I told the Units. "Really bad!"

They did too. They were old, long overdue replacement, and their pink outsides had turned a purply-brown.

Disconnection and chucking out, that was the first job. It was easy: disconnect one and that made the automatic system click in to do the rest.

I went for the closest Unit, the one on the middle row near the door, and pulled the output tube from its end. That was always the easy bit; Units never liked that tube. The input tube was more difficult; that was the feed tube and, though Units didn't have heads or brains, they clung to their food! I had to hold the hot, smelly Unit in one hand and pull the tube out with the other. There was a loud pop and I felt all the other Units give a shake. You couldn't see it or hear it, but you knew they all did it – an invisible shudder. Didn't bother me much at other times, but this day… It was a weird day. So I stood there wondering if all these Units knew they were about to be mashed to nothing and turned into feed for the next lot.

Then the floor started opening and I stepped back to the control panel. The tubes pulled free of all the Units and, seeing them there without their tubes, I suddenly thought of the dead Alien dropping from Mott's sack. Units looked just like it had looked! Just like a bird without its head or feathers! I watched them slide, as the shelves tipped and they fell into the pit under the shed. Were Units some sort of odd bird? Is that what birds were like on Home – headless, featherless and ugly?

After the floor closed over the old Units, jets of steam and cleaning stuff spurted from all directions, then hot dry air blasted in. In ten minutes the shed was bare; totally clean, as if there'd never been a thing in there. The conveyor door opened and the crates of new Units started rolling in. Mott was in charge of connections normally, but I was going to do it alone today. Connection was tricky. It made my hands sweat to think of getting it wrong. It would be more than Mott who'd be angry if I did. Fortay usually checked Product flow on new Unit connections. Ah, but not today, I remembered, and perked up.

I opened the first crate and began putting the new pink Units onto the conveyor. Their input holes opened and closed, and sucked at my fingers. I tried to remember what TV said about Units not really being alive, about being made in a factory on Home and brought here. But the white bird kept coming into my mind, alive and flying, then dead and slipping from Mott's sack, *looking just like a Unit*. I couldn't get the right beat to the work. Tubes kept tangling and misconnecting. Crates kept stacking up.

Then I saw it. Sticking out of the pink side of a Unit was a white feather! At first I thought it was the one from the Alien, which I'd stuffed in my pocket when I got up, but it was still there. I pulled it out and put it by this new feather. They were exactly the same. I pulled the feather on the Unit, but it wouldn't come loose. It was stuck right in the pink skin, growing there!

Then something inside me slipped. A small, small slip, like the first move at the top of a ramp, when you know in a second things'll slide so fast, you won't be able to stop them, no matter what. I knew somehow that everything had changed, inside me and outside too.

That's when I saw the delivery conveyor had stopped and everything had gone extra quiet. Suddenly the lights went out and a red ball exploded into the shed and blew me against the door. When I opened my eyes again, the whole shed was alive with fire – real fire. You couldn't tell from TV how greedy fire was, or how hot. Shelves and tubes were melting, Unit bodies going black, smoke and smell all over. I stood and stared at it all. All the normalness of the shed that I had worked in every day had gone wrong. It didn't seem real. I stood and stared, and it took a lick of flame on my hand to wake me and get me frightened enough to move. I got out, with the flame leaping after me.

I ran down the corridor from the shed and back to the body of the Station. There were no lights, just the day starting to come through the roof and the red of fire moving on the high walls all around. Voices came from the hangar where the delivery plane was; too many voices and too loud to be guards. And there were flat-sounding bangs and pops that I knew must be shots. I thought, *Rebels!* and all the TV stories about how they killed Workers and burned Stations came into my mind. Something big was happening; it had been coming towards me all the time and I hadn't seen it. *Seems you don't want to know nothing, though it's more than time you did!*

I started running to the hangar to find Mott. All the gates were open and fire was in all the old Unit sheds. I'd seen fire now and I knew it wouldn't stay there for long. Soon it would run out of things to eat and move on. Already the Station groaned and grumbled about the heat in its bones. The plane was still in the hangar, with both the inner and outer doors open. People – more people than I'd seen in a long time – were running up and down the ramp with boxes of stores: the delivery of Meals was being loaded back onto the ship!

I kept in the shadows. The people were Rebels, like the dead bodies on TV. They were rough-faced, scraggy-haired and armed, carrying blades of all sorts made from sharpened girders and bits of metal panels. More than half had Supas' guns, and some had body armour like Fortay. I crouched low and got to the other side of the inner doors, where it was darkest. Then I tripped over something. It was Fortay, lying stockstill. I stepped over him and almost trod on Mott. He was on his back on the floor. I got down beside him. His face was muzzy in the shadows, but I could see his eyes were open and still moving. "Mott! What's goin' on?"

"Rebels taking the Station. I let 'em in, but it's all wrong... They ain't *true* Rebels, Sacks." He grabbed at my sleeve and held on there without talking; just breathed and his breathing was bad, like metal scraping on a concrete floor. "That Hasp. He's done for me."

"Who's Hasp? What's the matter with you, Mott?"

His fingers grabbed mine in the dark. They were slack, with no iron in them now. He put my hand on his chest. There was a big wet hole there, sticky with blood. I could have put my fist in it. "No!" I pressed my hand over the hole, trying to block it, make it close. But more hot blood came up between my fingers. I'd said I hated him, but I knew then I'd never meant it. Mott had raised me from a little 'un. He'd been all I knew for as long as I could remember. I couldn't do without him. "Mott, don't die! Don't die!"

He pulled me down so my face was next to his and spoke in my ear. "This wasn't the plan. I was goin' to take you back."

"Back where, Mott?" I asked him, but I don't think he could hear me after that.

"My blade," he whispered, so quietly that I almost had to put my ear in his mouth to hear him. "My firemaker. And ... a paper. A *special paper*. Take 'em. Keep 'em safe." He patted his wet chest. "Here!"

I reached inside his overalls and pulled out a small pouch, no bigger than my spread hand, with stuff inside. I put it under my own clothes.

"That's it," he murmured. "'S'all you need."

A torch beam cut across us and a voice shouted from the dock. Mott pushed me away, but I wouldn't go. What would I do without Mott?

"Get out!" he wheezed. "*Don't let Hasp get you...* Get Outside. There's your Home, not some other piggin' planet!"

There were more voices. I got lower still, to be out of the way. I watched Mott's eyes close, and heard the last breath grind out of him. I wanted to stay there, but a shot smashed into the wall beside us, screaming on the metal and sounding all the way up to the roof. Was it this Hasp bloke and his mates trying to get me? I didn't wait to work it out. I just ran. Two men followed after me through the smoke. But I knew the Station and they didn't, so between me knowing and their firing, I lost them and hurried on.

There was fire almost everywhere now, all through the food stores and the old quarters. Only the far side, with my platform and Mott's door, was clear. Up on my platform there was just enough light to see by. I found a bag with a shoulder strap – an old tool sack. I put two big sheets of waterproof packaging in it because Outside was wet; more overalls because Outside was cold, a bottle of water because Outside was toxic, and the pouch Mott had given me because it was all there was left of him. I had no Meals to take, which meant the hunger was going to get me in less than a day. But there was nothing I could do about that, so I tried not to think of it.

Just then there was a noise below, on the ladder to the platform. A footstep, a voice. They'd found me. I didn't try being quiet; I wanted them to think they'd caught me by surprise. I walked across the platform, making my feet heavy, and picked up the brick light from beside my bed, then stepped into the lift, smoothly and quietly. I trusted they wouldn't guess an emergency battery worked it when the main power was down, so they might not guard the exit on the ground. I slid the door until it was almost closed. Then I got ready with the brick light, being very careful and slow, and sat listening.

They rushed the last bit of ladder, just like I thought they would. I saw the arm of the first man sticking up and threw the light clear across the platform, to hit it. There was a shout and a banging as one, or both, of them fell. Speedily I shut the door, put my hand in the lift slot and told it quietly, "Down".

The men were crashing about on the platform when I got to ground level. I slid open the lift door and the light from the roof came in, thin and grey. There, pressed into the corner of the lift, was the dark-haired pilot from the delivery craft. "Show me a way out," he asked. "Please. They're after me." He had Workers' overalls on, just like mine, and he looked scared. I suppose that's why I grabbed his hand and ran, without thinking any more about it.

Mott's door was far from the docking bay so the Rebels wouldn't see us as we left. I led the boy through it, then stood with my back on the Station wall, looking at Outside. All that

TV had ever said about Outside played in my head: the poisonous rain; the Alien beings – big ones that could kill you straight
off, or little ones that could creep into your ear at night and
eat you from the inside out. But that wasn't what frightened
me then. I'd been Outside and I hadn't been poisoned; I'd
seen Aliens and they hadn't wanted to kill me. It was the nothingness of Outside that made me afraid. Outside was blank. In
the Station there was a pattern: Meals One and Two to make
you feel right, and TV always telling you that you were part of
something big, which would take you where you *really*
belonged – to Home. Outside stretched on for ever. It didn't
give clues; it had nothing to tell you about what to do, or how
to be, or where to belong. Now I'd have to do and be without
Mott or the Station or TV telling me how and what. I wasn't
sure I could do it.

nero

THERE had been a lot of shooting, some of it at me. So the truth is, I wasn't thinking as well as usual. I felt pretty weak and fuzzy-headed. Otherwise I wouldn't have asked a *Worker* for help. What would have been the point after all I'd been told about them? "They are stupid, cowardly and selfish by nature," Father always said. "They consider only themselves. It is all they are capable of." And my daddy was always right. So when the young Worker took my hand and led me out, I didn't get it. Where was the "selfish" in that? It had to be the "stupid" coming out, because it was me the Rebels were chasing.

Whatever it was, at least I'd got away. The Rebels would assume I was trapped in the fire somewhere, safely fried. They'd leave with the craft and wouldn't look back. The thought of my *Uccello* in Rebel hands wasn't great, but while I was still breathing there was a chance I'd get her back. I stood outside the Station, looking out at the prairie, and tried to think what to do next.

Luckily for me and the Worker, our first decision was an easy one. The Station was about ready to blow. The wall behind us was buckling as the fire inside tore everything apart.

"It's getting hot," I told the Worker. Actually, this was quite an historic communication: my first with a real, live, flesh-and-blood Station Worker.

"Wha'?" said the Worker.

That sort of barely articulate mumbling was just what my father had led me to expect, so I tried again. This time I said it real slowly – and loud too, for good measure.

"The – wall – is – getting – hot. I – think – it – is – danger-ous – to – stay – here."

That worked. This time the Worker looked me right in the eye and replied, "I'm not stupid. You can talk plain."

My hand was grabbed again and we were running. Not in any particularly planned direction – "away" seemed good enough at the time. Then there was a kind of giant groan behind us and Station 27 stopped being Station 27 and became a pile of junk. Smoke and dust filled the air all around us, which was pretty lucky because the next sound was the roar of the *Uccello*'s engines overhead, flying low and looking for us, I guess, but nobody could see through that smoke. After a few moments she flew away, with her engines growl-ing and coughing in the hands of the untrained Rebel pilot.

Reality fell hard and sharp into the silence the craft left behind her. My big brother, Fortay, was dead. My craft, my glorious *Uccello*, was gone; flown off by some moron who would more than likely crash her. The big green prairie, which had seemed pretty exciting from the air, was plain scary at ground level.

OK. I have to confess that I lost it then. Father would not have been proud. I pretty much forgot about the Worker, so it was a shock when a hand reached out and wiped the wet on my cheek with a finger. I looked at the Worker's face properly for the first time and saw my rescuer was a *girl*, about my age, with dark, messy hair, smoky skin and black eyes. She made me uncomfortable. She didn't look like I'd expected a Worker to look. "Don't do that," she said softly. "'S'bad for you. Hurts."

Where had she learned *that* kind of behaviour? Workers were just one up from machines. "They have no sense of family," Father had explained. "They must be managed and controlled because they cannot think or feel as we do." I pushed her hand away and made myself think like a Supa again; like a real Nabisco, like Fortay. I mustered all the authority I could into my voice and said, "I'm OK now. I'll decide what to do."

I was sure she'd do as she was told. She'd run away from the Rebels after all. So it was clear that her co-worker, the wrinkly little guy who must have been their contact inside the Station, hadn't told her anything. She was still a reliable Worker – something I ought to be able to make use of. But it didn't even start to work like that. She stuck her chin out and looked me straight in the eye again. "Why d'you have to decide?" she challenged. "Why should I do what you say?"

She looked really angry. I guess going from blubbering idiot to almighty despot in an instant is a tad irritating. But I was angry now too. The straight facts were that she *was* the Worker and I *was* the Supa, and in our world she did what I said! "Because you're a Worker so you do what I tell you!"

"Oh yeah?" she said. I looked at her. She was bigger than me and I didn't have any kind of weapon. Even if I had, what did I really know about fighting? The only time I held guns was when I was fixing broken ones. I knew about making bombs and grenades, but using them? That was Fortay's department.

The girl didn't blink. She just looked right back at me, her eyes deep and alive, like a tunnel with a fire at the end. It made me uncomfortable again. How could a Worker – "little more than a machine" – have eyes like that? *OK*, I thought, *fine. I'll let you think you've won this time.* "So," I said, "what do *you* want us to do?"

"Dunno," came her flat reply. "Didn't want you telling me, is all!" And then she smiled, a big, big smile, and I had to look away because I wanted so hard to smile back.

Of course, she didn't have any ideas about what to do. How could she? She didn't know *anything*. Like all Workers, she was ignorant. She didn't know where the nearest Station was, or the City. Hah! Now I was winning! "We'll walk to Station 98," I said.

"Where's that?"

I'd travelled between Stations with Fortay, learning the piloting job. I knew how to fly the *Uccello* to most Nabisco Stations within three hours of the City; how to read the navigation system on board so that I could find them. But I didn't have a craft or a navigation system any more. I glanced around. The hangar side of Station 27 was directly behind us when we set a course for Station 98, so I knew the direction, sort of. "Over there!"

"How long will it take?"

I tried to answer fast, to look decisive. But actually, I had no idea. It was an hour, maybe two hours' flying time, depending on wind speed and how much fuel we wanted to burn. So that was around 400 miles. How fast was walking? Walking hadn't exactly been a big part of my life up until then; I moved in cars, in planes, in elevators. "Two days," I told her, as if I'd done it a hundred times. "Yes, two days."

She looked at her feet

I had thought two days sounded kind of manageable. Then I thought: *She's scared. She believes she's gonna get killed out here because that's what TV tells them to stop them running off! Two days'll seem like a lifetime to her.* So I told her "There's nothing toxic out here, not any more. No Aliens even. They're all … dead." I risked a smile.

"Well *that*'s not true!" she said.

"It is. Really. I'm a Supa – I know."

She stopped looking at her feet and did that chin-out thing again. "Oh yeah? Then why does TV say different then?"

This was *not* what I'd been led to expect from a Worker. "We *forgot* to change what TV said." That was a tactical error, admitting that Supas could make mistakes, but it was all I could think of.

She looked away and said something, just loud enough for me to hear. "Useless cack!" I hadn't heard that word before, but I knew that it must be an insult and that, as a Supa, I should take some sort of action against her. Yet it was *exactly* the sort of thing I'd wanted to say to my father sometimes, but had never had the guts. I had to turn my head away again, to stop her seeing my smile.

"We have to go this way," I said. "North-west." Then, to score a point back just the way I'd done with Fortay sometimes, I said, "You know about points of the compass?"

"What?"

Hah! There's no *way* she'd know the points of a compass from a hole in her head! "Useless cack," I said, and we smiled widely at each other and began to walk.

The prairie looked flat when we started. How hard could walking on the flat be? But it wasn't flat. There were lumps all over, and hills – sneaky hills – everywhere, that you didn't notice until your legs ached and your lungs hurt. The girl looked like she was coping OK. I guess Workers did more

walking than we did. I watched her striding up slopes in front
of me and wondered how the system had missed her, so that
even Fortay had thought a man and a boy ran Station 27. Why
had that wrinkly old guy done it? Was it part of his Rebel
ideals? Was there something special about this kid?

The sun got high and walking got hot. We both stopped
at the same time and sat down. The girl pulled a bottle out of
her bag and started to drink. I watched her. I didn't feel like
another fight so I couldn't order her to share it.

"Can I have some?" I asked.

She handed me the bottle without a word, and I drank
more of the water than I should have, but she didn't notice.
She was looking up at the sky. I guessed she was scared. The
open space of the prairie had to be pretty scary for a person
who'd never known anything outside the dome of a roof; it
was scary for me, and I'd flown over it willingly, excitedly, for
months. But when I passed the bottle back to her I could see
she wasn't afraid – not at all. She looked kind of lit up somehow, like she was taking everything in.

"Will the sky be like this on Home?" she asked. "As good
as it is here?"

I was caught in those slow-burning eyes and I didn't know
what to say. I'd seen a few of the Worker TV broadcasts about
Home, the planet that we're all *supposed* to be from; the
planet that TV talks a lot about, to make the drudgery of
Worker life seem OK. "On Home?" I replied, swallowing hard.

"Yeah. When we get Home I want to walk like this. Just walk and walk, under our *own* sky."

I didn't know what to say to that. I just had to remember to close my mouth. I'd thought – if I'd thought about it at all – that the Planet Home thing was a nice bit of comfort for the Workers; that it was simply like putting oil into a car to make it run. I didn't imagine that they'd be able to build dreams about it. After a minute I said, "The sky? Oh. Just the same!" But lying *for real* to someone you've met is a lot more difficult than lying from a distance to people you've never seen. I knew she didn't believe me.

She snatched the water bottle and put it back in her bag. "Got to make it last," she said.

We walked on and on. The white clouds tracked across the sky and the breeze made patterns in the grass. I kept wondering what the girl was thinking. Was the sameness of the prairie getting inside her head, like it was getting inside mine, making me feel that maybe my brain was made of green strands blowing in the wind? *Shut up!* I told myself. *Get a grip. This is a Worker here. That's all.* "You must never imagine that they are even worthy of a name. To you they are all as one, simply Worker. Units of a machine, to be used for our benefit." Why did Father have to be so pompous?

We'd been walking for hours so I guess a little drama at this point at least relieved the tedium. "Blood!" the girl said suddenly and pointed to my leg.

I looked down. Yeah, that was blood all right. My left trouser leg was wet with it, from the calf down. "Must have taken a bullet during the raid," I answered, and sank to the grass. *No big deal,* I told myself. In the City people got shot all the time. Since the Rebel raids on Stations and the feuds between the Supa families, Father's surgeon had been patching somebody up almost every day. I'd seen the bandages on my father's guards, my uncles even; clean white bandages, covering up any trace of red. Blood oozed out of my boot where it had collected, bright, sticky and red. I passed out.

When I came to, everything ached. I levered my eyes open, as if my eyelids were craft doors on manual. Looking down on me were faces; huge dark faces. They had big black eyes under thick curly brows, and curving growths from the tops of their heads. They almost touched me with their noses – as wide as my head – and their breath streamed out of their nostrils, hot and smelly, like the exhaust fumes from a big machine.

There was a gasp that wasn't mine, and I remembered the Worker girl and the hole in my leg. So I knew that this wasn't a dream. The girl was at my feet. She'd been sleeping too maybe and had woken to find the faces of what must be "strange Alien monsters" staring down at her; the nightmare TV had warned her about all her life!

But they weren't strange to me. I knew them very well. I'd

seen them before, running across my workshop wall and into my dreams. Fortay brought them to me from the old layers of the City, below the tenth floor. Down there, the region we called the "Low Tens", everything was solid with rubbish; ruined, flooded, dangerous. Our father hated it that Fortay went there. "Why do you go?" he'd say. "There's nothing down there but the dead past."

"And Rebel hiding places, Father," Fortay would answer back. "I want to know where to look when the time comes."

But I guessed it was more to do with what he found down there than Rebel hunting.

"Look at this, Nero," he'd say, dumping some broken piece of incomprehensible twentieth-century rubbish on my bedroom floor. I pretended to be angry, but we both knew I wasn't. I liked working out what that old stuff had been for. "Here," he said one day. "The label said 'cine projector'." He put a machine and two little flat silver cans on my floor. "Don't know what it is. See if you can work it out!" It took me a while. The cans had reels of pictures inside and if I fed them in the machine right, they came to life on my wall. There wasn't much, maybe forty seconds, a minute. Moving pictures of great bulky beasts running over wide grassy plains, then a little clip of some crazy old guy dancing and wearing the head and skin of one of the beasts. There was nothing familiar in the pictures; no streets or buildings. There was no sound, but there were words written on the screen at the end. They said:

They walk, they stand, they are coming.
Yonder, the buffalo are coming.

I guessed that those were the words the old guy was saying as he danced, and that the buffalo were the big brown animals running around. I watched it over and over, over and over. It occurred to me, after a while, that the buffalo pictures were taken a long time before the old guy's dancing, and that he was dancing on an empty prairie, just dreaming that he'd meet up with the buffalo some day. I asked Fortay what he knew about it. He said the guy and the creatures lived long ago. "The time 'before'," he said, "when there was all kinds of other life on Earth." I watched the film every night, looking out at the City, the lights and the buildings, and wondered where it had all gone, that life from "before".

Father took it all away in the end, the film and the projector; took it up to the roof and torched it. "If you want to mend something," he said, "then mend our weapons. Direct what small abilities you have to help the family." But the pictures still played in my head, in the darkness, when the City screamed outside. I thought about what it would be like to be that old guy dancing his dreams in a buffalo skin. I wished that he'd got his buffalo back and that they were both still alive somewhere. But I knew they couldn't be…

Until that moment when I woke to the big brown heads breathing their warm, grassy breath over my face. I looked into

51

their eyes for a long time. I wanted to make absolutely sure that I *was* awake. At last I sat up, and so did the girl. "Help me get up," I told her. No arguments this time. She just did it, and stood beside me. When we moved, the buffalo moved back, their feet dull-thudding on the ground. There were about twenty of them; huge mounds of brown fur balanced on dainty feet. They breathed at us *wufff, wufff,* and tossed their low, heavy heads with the shiny curves of their horns peeking through the curls of hair. I wanted to see them run, like they'd run in my head so many times. "Yahhh!" I yelled, and waved my arms. "Yahhhhh!"

They backed off, so I waved again and yelled some more, and they turned and began to lumber away. A great, rocking run, just the way I remembered it.

They walk, they stand, they are coming!
Yonder, the buffalo are coming!

The buffalo kept running into the distance, then disappeared out of sight over the brow of one of those sneaky hills.

I sat down, feeling shaky, and looked at the ground where they'd stood. There were marks in the dirt that their feet had made. It was true: they were real. And if buffalo were real, what else might be out there that we Supas had said was long dead? I shivered to think of it, with a kind of deep happiness and a kind of terrible fear.

The girl crouched in front of me. "What were they?" she asked, her face lit up again and her eyes burning.

Everything was right there in my mouth at that moment; the whole deal ... about Planet Home, about TV, about "toxic Aliens", about the old guy and his dancing. Right at that moment I would have told her the *whole truth* that I knew, but just one word came out.

"Buffalo." I said. "They're called buffalo." She didn't ask anything else and for a while we just stood and looked – dazed, I guess.

If my Father had overheard us talking then, after the buffalo had rumbled off, over the wide grass, I'd have made the excuse that I was tricking this Worker, getting into her confidence, in case of trouble. But it would have been a lie.

"What's your name?" I asked her.

"Sacks," she said, and looked back from the prairie to my face. "And you?"

"Me? Nero Nabisco, but Nero is fine."

She'd tied a piece of plastic rope round my leg to stop the bleeding, and had mopped up some of the blood with a handful of grass. So pretty soon we got walking again. The sun began serious sinking after that, turning the prairie purple and the sky red. We walked on, but I wasn't so certain about things now; about my plans for where we might be heading. There seemed to me to be other possibilities about what I might do next that I hadn't considered before. I even caught myself thinking that I might just stay out on the prairie with Sacks and see if the old guy's great-great-great-grandson turned up. *Nero*, I said to myself, *you sure have lost a lot of blood!*

I don't remember when exactly Sacks began to sweat and stumble. I knew what that was about, and at first I was irritated. She was being Worker-stupid not just to eat the Meal Two she must have with her. "You should eat your Meal, Sacks," I told her. "Supas don't have Meals like you do so I won't take it from you."

She looked at me, but her eyes had gone dull, the way I'd always thought Workers' eyes would be all the time. When she spoke, her words were blurry. "No Meal Two," she said, then looked at me again. "You got Meal Two?"

I couldn't believe she would have left the Station without making certain she had her next Meal with her. "Are you sure you haven't got one with you? Look in your bag."

She stopped walking and tipped everything out of her bag. The slow carefulness I'd seen in her all day was gone. She was clumsy and stupid, pulling and shaking everything, as if the tiniest fold could hold one of those chunky foil packets. "Looking," she declared. "Searching and looking. Meal Two! Meal Two!" At last she turned the bag inside out and threw it down. "No Meal!" she shouted. "No Meal!" She stood still and stared up at the first stars coming out. Maybe she was looking for Home up there. Then she fell, and lay twitching on the ground.

I knew why. Workers *had* to have Meals to stay alive. Not

for the food but for the Product that Supas had always put in them. My father had explained it to me. "Product helps Workers. It keeps them happy. Keeps their minds free of worry, of thoughts that might get in the way of their desire to work. And of course it makes them unwilling to leave their Stations."

I hadn't understood that last part so I'd just forgotten about it, until one night I overheard Fortay and Father. It was late and I should have been asleep, but I always stayed awake until I heard Fortay come in safe off patrol. Fortay and Father were shouting at each other – or rather Father was shouting. I could see them through the open door of his study, standing face to face over the shiny pool of the table top.

"I don't care how it happened," Father hissed. "Losing more men is simply your incompetence!"

That made me angry. There was nothing incompetent about my big bro! I almost stepped out of the shadows to defend him, but he didn't need it. He could cope with Father's rages and stay cool. He took a deep breath. "Look, sir, Father, it's simple: we can't afford any more Workers turning Rebel or becoming street fighters for rival families."

"And what do you suggest I do?"

"You *know* what needs doing. Double the levels of Product in Meals."

"It's too expensive."

"No, it's a sensible investment. With double the Product

dose they'll be so dependent that if they miss a single Meal, they could die. It'll slash the desertion rate. Rebel bands just won't be able to recruit any more."

A board creaked under my foot and they both looked up suspiciously. Fortay kicked the door closed, and I went back to bed.

Fortay's plan worked, I guess. Which is why he finally had time to teach me to fly the *Uccello*. I was a natural, he said. After five hours' air time, I felt I'd been doing it for ever. "You could be really useful, little bro … for a skinny kid!" Fortay told me. "In a month or two I might need you to do this for real, not just for fun!" I didn't care what it was for, so long as I was flying. We flew out to Stations far from the City, over wide, green prairies. I knew it was crazy, but all the time I looked out for the old guy and his buffalo.

I didn't care that we were feeding Workers a drug that was dangerously addictive. I didn't even think about it, until the moment when Sacks' eyes stared without seeing, and her hair stuck in wet strings to her head. *They'll be so dependent that if they miss a single Meal, they could die.* Sacks was going to die and I couldn't do a thing about it. I rolled her onto one of the packing sheets she'd brought with her, covered her with the other and tried to feed her a little water, but her teeth were clamped and chattering. I sat with my back to her, but I couldn't bear the sound of her tossing and turning in her stiff, rustling covers. There was just enough light left to walk away, far enough not to see or hear her. But alone in the dusk, all there was inside my head was me, and I didn't want to see that. I found my way back to Sacks and sat beside her.

It got cold, then colder. I crept under the sheet with her. Her body was burning now and the glow of it kept me from freezing. One of Father's little mottoes floated back to me out of the dark: *We take from Workers who are capable of so little because we are capable of so much.*

Not that Father had ever thought *me* capable of very much. And right then, lying beside Sacks' shaking body, I'd never felt less capable in all my life. All I could think was she was going to die because of what Supas had done; all I could do was look up at the dark sky and watch the stars moving slowly, slowly, from one horizon to the other.

My mind wandered to where I hadn't let it go all day: to Fortay. Fortay leaning in the frame of the hold door, with his right arm shattered, reloading one-handedly. "Don't argue, Nero," my brother had whispered. "Just do as I say! We've been set up here, and there's nothing we can do about it. Just get out and run ... now!"

I'd slipped out of the cargo doors and run through the smoke. A single shot had sounded behind me, and a man's voice had shouted out, "Got him! But I want the other one alive!" I'd looked back at the *Uccello*. Rebels were already loading the Meal cartons back on board, as if nothing had happened.

Meals! Meals! My mind snapped back to the present, and Sacks. The Rebels had Meals! I sat up straight, suddenly absolutely sharp, not tired at all any more. They'd arrived at the Station without a craft, so they couldn't have travelled that far. Their camp, or hideout or whatever, had to be round here somewhere! I got out from under the sheet and felt around in the pathetic pile of belongings from Sacks' bag. I opened an odd little pouch. Inside, among various bits of junk, was something that looked like a firemaker. I pressed the button on the firemaker's side, not really expecting anything, and a tiny flame sprang out. *Well, look at that*, I thought. I gathered some dead grass and set light to it. It crackled and burned up and I fed the flame again, more this time; more and more until there was a fat column of white smoke snaking up into the sky and blotting out the stars.

sacks

THE fire was hot and greedy. I thought I'd be swallowed up in it like all the Units in the shed, like Mott and the Station. And I was glad because the pain of wanting a Meal was that bad. I shut my eyes.

But the fire didn't eat me. When I opened my eyes, it had got small and was held behind a ring of stones. I was inside, but not like any inside I knew. The walls were made of packing and old carpet, held up with bits of girders from Station walls. The roof was pointed, and had a hole that showed the night sky of Outside between the breaths of smoke. I was lying on a low bed, with a blanket made of overalls sewn together on top of me. I felt empty, like a blank space, with no past or future; only this moment and the safe warmness of the bed.

A woman leaned over and looked down at me. Her face was worried and crumpled-looking, and her brown hair stuck out from a knot on the top of her head. She wore patched overalls but her arms were bare, and banded with braids of coloured wire. "So, are you all right then?" She spoke like a

Worker, up and down, not flat like a Supa.

"I dunno," I croaked, which was true enough, because I didn't know what I was, OK or not.

"You hungry?" she asked.

"I dunno," I said again, and that was true too. I wasn't sure if what I was feeling *was* hunger. It wasn't a hungry feeling that I recognized.

The woman smiled and her face uncrumpled. I saw that she wasn't much older than me. "I know what you need," she declared. "Food. Not *Meals*, just *food* – without what the Supas puts in it to keep us stupid. Here!"

I didn't know what she was going on about, but I took the bowl of green goop and the bent spoon to eat it with.

"It's Supas' food," she said. "What they eat. It's made from weed, after it's put through some machine or other. Anyways, we took it off a Station what was makin' it. We've loads – enough for months!"

I ate, and she stood with her arms folded, watching me. I wiped my finger around the bowl until it was clean of every scrap.

"Well?" she said, smiling again. "How was that?"

I didn't have any words for how it was, but I knew how it made me feel. "Good," I answered, and smiled back at her.

She took the empty bowl and sat on the bed. I could feel her weight and warmth next to me. It was strange to be so close to a woman. "It don't have no Product in it, is why," she told me, making the word Product sound like "poison". "Our leader says 'Product is a chain, binding Workers to what Supas wants!'" The way she said it made me think of an electronic voice chanting, "Meal One! Gets your day's work done!" Meals. Product. Units. Stations. Supas ... Mott. But she talked on and I listened. "Product isn't just food. The Units is bred, special, to make Product with something else in it. A drug. It's what makes you lively in the morning and makes you sleepy after TV at night. Makes you stupid too *and* it makes you forget stuff. Once you've had Product, you can't do without it. That's why you get so hungry for it!"

I nodded sadly, remembering now how I'd stood outside the Station whimpering for my Meal.

"Product takes you over!" she went on. "It's worse now. They put more Product in Meals, so's Workers will die for *sure* if they don't get it. It makes people scared to leave Stations and join us."

"But I didn't die," I said.

She shrugged. "If you get through the first two days, you'll live. Most don't, specially not now. Near everyone dies, unless they get off Meals slow, little by little. There's Workers here, four years off Station and still needin' a bit of Meal to live. You're just lucky."

I didn't feel lucky, only sad. I was remembering Mott. Mott and his roasted birds. Mott who was able to go without Meals. Mott with a hole in his chest on the floor of the burning Station.

"You didn't know any of that, did you?" asked the woman, more gently than she'd said anything. I shook my head. "Your Mott was one of us. Didn't he tell you anything?"

"Not so's I'd understand."

She nodded. "I heard he was a weird old boy. I 'spect he had his reasons."

I felt tired again. *So* tired. I laid down.

"You rest now," the woman whispered softly. "You'll soon be feeling strong." I shut my eyes. Somewhere above me, she was still speaking. "We're all goin' to Home soon. To Planet Home. You wait and see." But there were no dreams of Home left inside me. They'd washed them out of my body with the drug of Product and the Supas' lies.

Next time I opened my eyes it was daylight. The fire had given up and died behind its little wall. I was cold, and watery-weak, with my thoughts washing and twining like weed floating in a tank. I remembered Nero; Nero lying about the sky on Home; Nero saying "buffalo" like it was the truest word he'd ever spoken. He was tangled up in my anger at the Supas and all their lies. Yet he didn't fit in with other Supas; not in his looks or in the way he spoke. I wondered where he was and began to fear for him among the Rebels. But loud noises outside ended my thinking. First there was a banging, like an empty Meal carton being hit hard and steady, *Wack!* *Wack!* It moved around, left to right, near and far. I heard voices calling out to each other:

"C'mon."

"It's time."

"Over here!"

"Get on, Ratchet!"

"Dunn! Get over here!"

"Kedd! You coming or what?"

"Coil! Coil! Hurry up."

"Come on, Hasp's going to speak!"

I heard the name and shuddered, as if Mott's hot blood was between my fingers again. *That Hasp. He's done for me,* Mott whispered out of the air.

Suddenly the banging stopped and the voices too, and just one voice – sharp, hard as a blade – sliced into it; Hasp's voice.

"Friends!" he announced. "You know the lies that Supas have told you –"

Yesses came from every side.

"And the biggest lie of all is how Supas are working to take *all* of us to Planet Home. Well, here's the truth: *you* work and *they* go Home!"

There was more crate-bashing after that, so it was a while before Hasp spoke again.

"Today is a great day!" He didn't sound like a Worker, nor like a Supa, but something in between. "Today, I have good news: we are on our way Home, as I have always promised you!"

"Home! Home! Home!" all the other voices called out.

I'd never heard such excitement. All those voices chanting together, as if Planet Home was parked right out there and all they had to do was hop on.

"We are going Home because we have captured the Supa aero-craft and its Nabisco pilot."

The Workers fairly roared, and there had to be a bit more crate-banging to calm them again.

"Nabisco – the greatest of all Supa families – are leaving for Home very soon. Their spacecraft is ready."

There was no yelling from the crowd now; nor even a whisper. The words dropped into a deep quiet.

"We have captured the Nabisco's youngest son," Hasp explained. "In return for his safety, he will take us, in the captured aero-craft, to the borders of the City. With Nero Nabisco in our power, Supas will give us safe passage to the Nabisco space rocket and to our journey Home. He is our passport and our guide!"

For a little while there was no sound, as if all the people out there had just disappeared to nothing. Then noise exploded: screaming, shouting, crying, laughing ... everyone celebrating the fruit trees, the oceans, the blue skies, the *belonging* of going Home.

All around my bed was silence. I wanted to feel like the Workers outside; but I didn't. I was afraid. *Don't let Hasp get you,* Mott had said. *Get Outside. There's your Home, not some other piggin' planet.* Yet here I was, under Hasp's roof, the only one to feel the empty lie in all his plans. The weight of it pressed me down and pushed me under.

I woke a long time later and watched the light come in at the roof hole, and listened to the sounds coming through the tent. Not the creaks and clanks of the Station walls, nor the chatter of TV, but the sounds of Outside: wind and silence, voices talking in their own time. It calmed me and made Mott's voice fade.

Remember, Mott, you're a freak, I told him in my head, and felt better.

When it got really light the woman came again, with another bowl of the green food. She sat on the bed while I ate. "What's your name then?" she asked.

I answered without looking up. My name was nothing to me, but it seemed to mean more to her. "Sacks? Is that right?" she asked. "You always been called that?"

"Mott called me other names when he was angry. But you don't want to hear them!" I looked up from my food, but she wasn't smiling.

"Sacks?" she persisted. "You sure?" Her mouth was as straight and tight as a zip.

A thread of fear tightened in me, and Mott's voice pushed into my mind. *They ain't true Rebels.* "I ain't too stupid to know my own name!" I blurted out, but still she didn't smile. She rubbed her bare arms as if to warm them and wouldn't look in my face. "What's *your* name then?" I asked.

"I'm Flame."

"You sure?" I teased. She looked at me then all right, but not to smile.

"Come with me," she said, sharp as a blade. "Outside, if you can walk."

It took a moment to see anything more than the bright light. Then I saw the green prairie under the sky, which was patched in blue and grey. I'd been inside a big, cone-shaped tent and all around were more – fifteen or so. All of them had clothes and tools stacked outside on the grass. I knew some of the tools: a big gas welding kit like the one Mott kept near the docking bay, and a small lifting machine like the one we used in the store room. But there were other tools I didn't know, made of all sorts: bits of wall and cut-up crates. There were people everywhere: the Rebels I'd seen on the day Mott was killed were busily moving about as if were working on a Station. They looked at us as we walked by. A few nodded or smiled at the woman, but then looked straight through me as if I were glass.

We walked out of the ring of tents onto the open grass. A wind was moving through it and blowing into our faces. Above us, the sky was busy too; great lumps of grey were shifting without a sound, changing places with the blueness. I was staring at it so hard that I almost fell into the water when we came to it.

"'Ere's where we get our drinking water." Flame pointed

beyond the surface of a big pool, about the size of the Station 27 hangar, to the place where it squeezed between two close rocks then ran away down a little slope. "And down there, where it goes out and away," she continued, "that's where we can wash and do our business. It in't toxic. Leastways nobody died yet!" At last she smiled and looked at me. "Go on," she urged. "Go down there. Don't look to me like you're strong enough to run off!" She gave me overalls, Station issue and the wrong size as usual, but clean.

It seemed strange to wash in water straight from Outside – and cold. I shook from the chill and weakness of my body. Flame was right. However feared I was of Hasp, I couldn't go anywhere until I was stronger. I took off my clothes and stood on a rock at the edge of the flowing water. I used the pot that Flame had given me to pour water over myself until I was clean. Then I stood to dry in the air, naked among the waving grasses under the great moving sky. Earth below, sky above and me there in between, small and soft. I felt something that wasn't fear or hurt but just as strong and much, much bigger. Then Flame called, "Be quick! I'm sure 'tis going to rain!" I heard the alarm in her voice so I put on my clothes and went to her.

Rain was the most fearful thing Outside, according to TV. Any drop of it might carry poison to hurt you. "How can the water be safe if the rain is toxic?" I asked.

"I don't know," Flame replied, "but I don't want to find

out." She ran ahead, back to the tents. I could see all the other Rebels running too, eager for shelter, but I couldn't run. I walked slowly, and when I came to the settlement the Rebels stood in their dry doorways and watched me. The drops fell on my head and neck, and I turned up my face to catch them. They landed on my lips and on my eyelids, soft and cool. If one part of what Supas had told us was lies, then it was *all* lies. I *knew* the rain wouldn't hurt me. I *knew* that all I believed now was my eyes and my ears, my fingers and my feet, and the thoughts in my own head. I sat outside the tent, looking at the big sky and the wide prairie; at the colour of the clouds, the pattern of shadows on the grass, and the ripples on the lake's surface. I thought of birds, covering me with white wings, and of Nero's buffalo, running heavily over the purple grass to make the ground shake.

Later, Flame came back. She smiled when she spoke and met my eyes. Whatever had been bothering her earlier was gone. I wanted to try and ask where Nero was, but there wasn't space for anything in her talk, which was all about Planet Home, and how Nabisco's rocket ship would take us there, just like the rocket ships they showed on TV. I breathed deeply and looked out at the grass. She told me her name had been Circuit before, when she'd worked on Station 62, but she'd been free for two years now and didn't want the name from her old life. "Why don't you change your name when you gets Home?" she suggested.

"You got a right thing about names!" I said.

"New name for a new life! Most folk say they'll change names on Home."

"But I'm not going Home." I said it without a thought, and it was only when it was out in the open that I knew how true it was.

Flame looked at me with wide eyes. "What d'you mean, *not going*?"

"I'm not going. How do we know Planet Home is real?"

"'Cos TV shows it! 'Cos Hasp says we're going there..." Flame seemed ready to cry. "Because we don't belong here."

"I do," I said. "I reckon I belong right here."

"You're crazed!" she exclaimed, "real crazed!" Then she got up, and left.

I slept until the evening, and when Flame came with my bowl of food she wouldn't smile or look at me. She just said, "Hasp wants to see you. C'mon. You can walk, can't you?" I let her lead me to a tent with a silvery door that reflected the pink evening sky.

"In here," she gestured, and pushed me forward.

Inside, some light came through the thin tent walls, making a sort of glowy shade. A man sat in a wide black chair. Only his pale hands and narrow white face showed up; his mouth a small, dark hole. "Your name's Sacks?" he asked.

I knew that voice, like sharp metal. I nodded.

"D'you know my name?"

"You're Hasp."

"Yeah. That's right. Hasp-sir to you, girl. Did you hear what I said?"

"Yeah," I said, with no more sound in my voice than a breath.

"Yeah what?" Another voice spoke from behind me and a big hand dropped onto my shoulder so that my knees shook. Hasp had a guard, just like the ones the Supas had! "Yeah what? Yeah, Hasp-sir, that's what you say!" the guard growled.

"Yeah, Hasp-sir," I repeated. The hand stayed clamped on my shoulder.

"Better!" said the guard.

"You've been telling everyone that there isn't a Planet Home," Hasp went on. "That Planet Home is a lie." His voice was quiet, but still it made my skin go cold.

"No, I haven't," I denied. "I only told Flame I wasn't going Home."

"And why is that, Sacks?" Hasp leant forward in his chair, and I couldn't help but step back. He scared me.

"I don't believe any Supas' lies, that's why."

"Planet Home isn't a lie, Sacks. Planet Home is what my Rebels *live* for. If I hear you've been saying such things to *anyone*, you'll be in big trouble. *Big* trouble." His voice didn't change; still quiet, without anger, but the quietness terrified me more than shouting ever could. "I'm not at all pleased with you, Sacks. But you could make me pleased." He motioned to the guard to leave and didn't speak again until we were alone. "You could tell me something about you and Nero," he said eventually.

"I don't know nothin' about him, Hasp-sir," I replied.

"Nothing? *Nothing?* Why d'you help him get out of the Station then?"

"He asked!"

"Don't give me lip, Sacks. You've known each other for a long time, haven't you?"

"He's a Supa. How could I know him?"

"Look, girl, I think I know who you are, see? Who you *really* are. Who Nero *really* is. And if you cooperate with me, we could do a *very* nice little deal. But if you don't, I could kill both of you now, and it wouldn't matter that much."

Hasp got out of his chair and pushed me to the ground, then he put his big boot on my head. The metal studs dug into the side of my face. "Tell me about you and Nero. Tell me your old names. Your *real* names."

"You're a freak, Hasp," I gasped. "I don't know what you're on about."

He leant harder on my face. "I wonder how strong your head is, *Sacks*? If I stamped on it now, what d'you reckon would happen?" He was nearly standing on my head. "Why don't you just say your name? I know it anyway. You wouldn't be telling something I don't know."

How would it be when my head cracked? Would it smash in one go and make me dead, or would it break a little at a time?

"How did you and Nero keep in touch? Who else have you contacted?"

Hasp was mad. Demented. What did I know about Nero? A lot of lies and one true word: *buffalo*! If my end was going to be here, I wanted to be thinking of something good. So I listened for the sounds of Outside coming through the thin tent walls. Human voices, wind; people walking free under the wide sky. Then, faint and far at first but coming closer, was the language of the white birds. Calling and answering, they flew right over Hasp's roof. I stopped feeling the studs piercing my skin. I stopped hearing the fear shouting inside me. I wasn't scared any more. My face was half-crushed into the ground and it was hard to speak, but all the same I shouted out, "My name is Sacks. That's ALL. So kill me and get it done with!"

Hasp took his boot away and I opened one eye. He was laughing. I jumped up and spat at him, and it hit him right in the face. I was so angry, I didn't think to be cautious. But he only wiped away the spit and laughed more.

"Well, that's as good as saying your own name. It'll do for now."

He got me by the shoulder, and held me so that my ear was by his mouth.

"Here's what we'll do," he hissed. "You'll be Nero's keeper, his watcher. He does something I don't like, you're dead. And you do any more blabbing about Planet Home, he gets the bullet, then you, clear? OK? Now get out."

He called in the guard, and I was put into a sack and dragged off. "Sack's in a sack!" called Hasp, laughing loudly at his own joke.

The bag was pulled off my head and I was in the cockpit of the aero-craft, the *Uccello*, where I'd seen Nero and Fortay standing the day Mott was killed. That all seemed like a very long time ago. The window was covered with a cloth, so we couldn't look out. Did Hasp and the Rebels believe that Nero and I were some sort of spies?

Inside and close-up, the cockpit was much bigger and less shiny and neat than I'd thought it would be. The control desk – all lights and switches and the black marks Supas called "writing" – was greasy. Bits of wrapping, boxes of spares and tools lay scattered all over. Mott would've had a fit if I'd left our loading bay like that!

Nero's boot and bandaged leg stuck out from under the desk – the rest of him was somewhere behind it. Two young Workers crouched beside his foot in a mesh of wires, holding torches and tools. They were mumbling away to each other and didn't see us, so the guard coughed and spoke through his helmet.

"Oi!" he said. "This 'un's from Hasp. He says she's gotta stay with Nero. I'm puttin' extra guards on the exit."

"Right," replied one of the Workers.

"Yeah! Right!" joined the other, but neither of them looked up, and went on fiddling with wires. It seemed that not everyone in the settlement was afraid of Hasp's thugs.

The guard waited for a moment, but when no one paid him any attention, he just shrugged and walked off, spluttering. As soon as he'd gone, one of the Workers stood up. He was round-faced, pale and ill-looking with dark spiky hair. He was short and slightly younger than me, I guessed. I thought that Mott might have looked something like him when he was young.

"You're the one we brought in with the Supa, aren't you?" he asked. "From the Station we raided?"

I nodded without speaking. My head was hurting and I couldn't think.

Now the other Worker stood up. The arms and legs on this one's overalls had been rolled over and over so as to fit their tiny limbs; their body was lost somewhere in the folds of material. "Look at the state of her, Rivet," this little one said to the first.

I could tell from the voice that this was probably a girl, though her head was inside the hood of her over-sized overalls. She pointed at me with small, red-wrinkly hands that had a sort of unfinished look to them. "Look at her!" she exclaimed.

I felt the side of my own face. There were deep dents, where Hasp's boots had dug in and made me bleed. The little red-handed Worker seemed very angry about it.

"Look at what that Hasp's done to her," she said to the boy. "Don't tell me about him being a great leader."

"Shuddup, Scanner. You don't know who's listening," hissed the boy, looking out of the cockpit into the corridor to the hold. "As long as Hasp gets us to Planet Home, he can do what he likes!"

Scanner scowled at him. "Well, that's nice, isn't it Rivet?" she said, then looked at me. "What did he do to you, girl?"

"Nothing much, I'm all right."

Scanner pushed her hood back and looked up at me. "Sure? Don't *look* all right."

I nodded. "But I'll sit down, if that's OK."

The spiky-haired boy, Rivet, pushed a box of tools off one of the pilot's seats, and swung it round for me. I fell into it and sat there while the two of them stared at me and I stared back. Scanner *was* a girl, for sure, but whatever had made her hands red had made her face too. Red as blood, it was, and crossed with a thousand tiny folds. Even the top of her head was red and wrinkled, where it showed between little clumps of chopped yellow hair.

"Got this from mending Supas' craft," she explained, running her hand over her cheeks, as if touching might make it better. "Standing in that hot engine blast all day and night shrivelled me up." Then she smiled, and all the creases in her face lined up so that her whole skin was smiling. "Yeah, I was blasted till the depot was raided, and the Rebels sprang me and Rivet out. Now we can mend craft for *us* to fly!"

"I never worked round the back end," added Rivet, "not like Scanner. So I never got the heat like she did. Hydraulics is my thing – doors and landing gear and that. You know about craft?"

I shook my head. "Unit Station all my life," I explained. "I know about circuits, though – electrics, loading-bay controls, communications…"

Scanner blew her cheeks out. "Well, that *might* be a bit of use…" She didn't sound convinced.

"Or it might not," said Rivet. "What'd Hasp send you up here for?"

I shrugged. Explaining what I'd been sent for, and how I wasn't going to do it, could get me into all sorts of trouble. "Dunno. 'Cos Nero and me was brought in together, 'spose."

A curse came from where Nero must have been, smothered by the wires and the desk and all. Rivet and Scanner looked at each other, then at me. Scanner held a finger to her lips and beckoned for me and Rivet to lean in close to her. "So," she whispered, "what d'you reckon to him?"

"I dunno," I said.

"Whaddya mean 'dunno'?" Scanner looked riled. "You still on Meals or what?" she snapped at me.

"Thanks, Scanner," whispered Rivet. "Just remember who *is* still on Meals round 'ere," and patted a tiny foil pouch, sticking out of his overalls pocket.

"Sorry, Rivet. You're nearly off, anyway. You know what I mean. She's playing stupid."

"I'm not," I protested. "I dunno about him. We got out of the Station together, is all."

"I heard you two was *special* or something."

I shook my head.

"What's the matter with you, girl?" Scanner growled.

For a small person, she could be scary. I thought I'd better say something, but I couldn't say what I really thought – which was that Hasp was up to something and that Planet Home was a load of rubbish. So I said, "Look, Hasp gave me a beating. I'm just a bit out of it, is all."

"Right. Course. Sorry," said Scanner. "But he seems *willing*, that Nero. Like he wants to do it. Like he really is *on our side.*"

"Give it up, Scanner," mumbled Rivet. "Let's just get the job done, eh?"

We turned back to the control desk just as Nero crawled out from under it. He looked bigger somehow, lit up with energy. "Hi," he said.

I nodded back. "Hi." I wasn't sure what to say to him, not sure which bits of him to believe in. But whatever I thought, for as long as Hasp was around, our lives were hooked together.

"This was our problem," Nero explained to Rivet and Scanner. "Main power circuit breaker, on a twenty-four hour delay." He held up a tiny circuit box, with its fine silver wires cut and ripped. "Fortay must have slapped it in there before the raid in case he didn't make it."

I remembered Fortay, lying with half his head blown away. I looked at Nero and wondered if he'd seen his brother like that too.

"He was smart my big brother," he said. "But not as smart as me. Oh no." And he gave a little whooping sound that made Scanner and Rivet laugh. Nero's mouth lifted at the corners. Was he smiling inside or crying? I wasn't sure.

nero

I found the stuff Fortay had stashed, including the circuit
breaker, almost as soon as I got behind the cockpit panel. I
held the little box and its snipped-off wires in my hand, and
thought about my big brother crawling about in there. He was
twice my size in all directions, so it would have been a tight
space for him to fit in, and connecting up the breaker would
have been awkward and time-consuming. He certainly hadn't
done it on the morning of the raid. He must have known that
there might be trouble well in advance.

I tried to remember if Fortay had said or done anything different on that morning, but it was hard. I was always pretty
wired before flight, and all I paid any attention to was getting
into the air and staying up there for as long as possible. But I
did remember a couple of weird things: one was that Father
had come to the hangar. He'd never done that before. I saw
him by the rear doors with his body guards, speaking to my
brother, but when I next glanced up from checking the fuel
line, Fortay was standing over me, just about ready to explode.

"He refused to give me extra men!" he snarled.

I liked it when Fortay got mad with Father, so I looked over to where the knot of guards was just disappearing and said, "Whoa there, *Dad*," – I *never* called him Dad to his face – "you're slipping! The *Uccello* isn't armed like the *Mandraya*."

Fortay stopped scowling and grinned. "Yeah... *And* he's forgotten that I have my own sources of intelligence."

Then the second weird thing happened: Fortay ruffled my hair! "Get your armour on today, little brother. OK?" he said.

Then we got ready for take-off, and I forgot about everything except that I, Nero Nabisco, was pilot of the *Uccello* on a real assignment. The fact that today, maybe, there was a little extra danger, was just another part of the game.

What had Fortay known about that morning that I hadn't? I gripped the circuit breaker tightly and tried to feel my brother's touch on it. But I couldn't. I understood now that we'd been playing different parts of the game. My part was my workshop: guns in pieces, the little wires and timers, trips and booby traps of explosive devices (I hated to call them bombs); like a never-ending set of puzzles to solve. Fortay's game was down on the streets, where anything might come at him out of the darkness. I'd never given much thought to the fact that he *used* the stuff I made and mended. And then, when we flew together, *he* had an objective: a delivery to make, intelligence to gather. All *I* wanted was to fly the *Uccello*. But still, for both of us it had been a game. Rebels were just bodies to count,

Workers just dots on a board. The only real part for me had been Fortay and the bird he had taught me to fly, the *Uccello*. The only way I could think of to make myself feel better was to get the *Uccello* back. I was clever enough to think of a way to do it, but was I tough enough to carry out a plan? Action had been Fortay's part of the game.

I hadn't had much of a plan when I lit the fire. It would attract the Rebels, Sacks would be saved and *somehow* I'd be sort of heroic and just fly off with my ship, leaving her with her Rebel mates to do their thing. Like I said, not much of plan. Pretty much based on how smart I was, and how "stupid" Worker Rebels would be. But the Rebel party who picked us up – three guys, plus a boy called Rivet and this tiny girl called Scanner – didn't match my expectations. They were fit and they were clever. I was impressed. I had a whole day of fast marching (and they marched fast, even carrying Sacks and with me blindfolded) to work out that just "flying off' wasn't that realistic an idea.

And then they took me to Hasp. I was dangled between a couple of thugs the size of Cadillacs and my blindfold was taken off. He was pale and wiry, dressed in close-fitting green overalls and a Supa's flak jacket. He walked around and around me, without saying a word at first; just smiling, as if I were his favourite meal or something. Apart from that weird smile, there didn't seem to be much that was special about him. And then he spoke. The voice was special all right. Not loud, but with an edge to it that parted the air. It drew your attention like a gun barrel pointed at your face. I recognized it at once from the Station raid: *"Got him! But I want the other one alive!"*

He was the guy who pulled the trigger on my brother. OK. So what? He was a Rebel; killing Supas was his job. No point taking that stuff personally. But Fortay had been injured. He could have been taken alive. I took one look at this guy, this Hasp, in the big chair he'd ripped from some piece of Supa machinery, and knew he'd do anything to get his way; he just liked winning. I realized then that I didn't have a single idea in my head about how to get myself out of this situation.

As it turned out, Hasp had plenty of ideas of his own. He got rid of his guard so he could share them with me, in private. "Looks like you risked a lot to save your little girlfriend," he goaded. "So you must know who she is."

"Sacks. She's called Sacks."

"Is she? What's she *really* called, Nero?"

"She told me her name was Sacks."

"How often did you two get in touch?"

"I don't know what—"

"Who else did you two contact? Hmm? Anybody important?"

I didn't bother to reply. He wasn't going to listen. He seemed pretty convinced that Sacks was a Supa spy, or something. And maybe she was, but I didn't know anything about it. So I shut up. He got nasty in the end, and I got very scared. By the time the guards dropped me down the hole behind his "business premises", I had a lot of bruises and even less of an idea about what to do than I'd had before.

I lay there feeling lousy and bruised, going over and over everything in my head: Hasp's questions, the booby trap in the cockpit, and Fortay endlessly saying, in my head,

We've been set up...

And I was still doing that the next day when I heard Hasp making his big speech. About me being their passport to the Nabisco spaceship and how the big leader, Hasp, was going to take them all to Planet Home! Pah! I was actually a little disappointed that the Rebels fell for it, but I guess Planet Home had been pumped into them by TV all their lives, so it wasn't so much of a surprise that they believed Hasp's story.

But Hasp didn't believe it. He didn't even seem to believe that I was Nero Nabisco. He knew that there was no spaceship that there wasn't even any Planet Home – and that if he set off with an aero-craft full of Rebels to find one, he'd soon look foolish. So why tell them all that stuff?

I lay there, still thinking, but all that came into my head now were pieces of junk; all the weird stuff that Fortay had trawled from the Low Tens over the years...

"Jewellery?"

"Nope."

"Some kind of weapon?"

"Nope."

"Come on, Fortay. You can't keep saying 'Nope'. You don't know what these are."

"Actually, just this once, I do."

He was really tired, and that was good. He was mellow when he was tired. He lay on my bed with the little box on his chest and with one of the curved pointed pieces of metal, the size of your thumbnail, on his palm.

"OK, so what?"

"It's to catch fish."

"Fish? What the hell are 'fish'?"

"Creatures. They lived in the water. About so big..."

I started to laugh, and so did he. He was winding me up, I knew it. "So how does a little bit of metal catch a creature the size of an automatic rifle?"

"Bait," he explained. "You use bait. That's some food the fish like. And you put it on here, on the point. And then you tie a string here, through the little loop part, and you throw it in the water."

"Sure!"

"And the fish takes the bait and the hook. They're called hooks – did I say that? And you pull the string and the fish is caught in the mouth, on the point."

He'd stopped laughing. He'd gone quiet and serious. It wasn't a wind-up. It was something else.

"I know," he said, very quietly, "because your mom told

me. It was something her family used to do long, long ago she said."

My mom had been Dad's third wife. Fortay was ten when they married and he really liked her. But my mom, like Fortay's, had died young. Although we never spoke of it, Fortay and I both knew that being married to my father was a death sentence. It was no surprise that nobody after my mother took the job.

"She told me she'd been fishing when she was a kid..."

He wanted to tell me more but my father's voice broke in.

"Fortay? Fortay!"

"I'd better go," Fortay said, but as he got up he whispered, "Hooks and bait. Remember, hooks and bait!"

That was it! The fish was this group of Rebels. The hook was the *Uccello*, and the bait was the Nabisco rocket and the promise of a passage Home. When Hasp had got all the Rebels on the hook, inside the *Uccello*, somebody would pull the string, to reel in the fish. So if I stuck close to the hook and the bait, I'd find the person who'd set up the raid and tipped off the Rebels that the virtually unarmed *Uccello*, and not the five-gunned *Mandraya*, was making the trip to Station 27.

When Hasp's thugs came to get me, that's as far as I'd got anything worked out. There was a problem with the *Uccello*, they told me, and I had to sort it out or I'd be "dead meat". "Mess up and your little friend Sacks will get a bullet too," they said. Great. I'd been a pilot for nearly a year and I knew the *Uccello* like I knew my own body. But knowing her as a mechanic? I was only a beginner.

Anyway, when they took the bag off my head, in the cockpit, my heart was beating so fast that I thought it would show through my clothes. It beat a little slower when I saw Rivet and Scanner; at least they were familiar. They didn't notice the heartbeat, but they did see the bruises.

"What 'appened to you?" asked Rivet quietly.

Scanner was bit more upfront. She stood in front of the thug, barely up to his waist, with her hands on her skinny hips and shouted at him, "Did you do that?" I thought he might hit her. But he actually looked embarrassed, as much as you could tell from the bits of his face visible under the black head gear. I couldn't believe that this tiny person was standing up for a prisoner she'd brought in; a Supa, an enemy.

"Professional interrogation techniques," the thug said. Scanner spat on the floor at the guard's feet, but he just shrugged. "Spit all you like. If the boy can't fix it, then Hasp-sir says he's dead. There'll be guards on the exits." He was definitely anxious to leave, and Scanner and Rivet seemed just as anxious to see him go.

"Hi!" I said, trying to sound relaxed and earnest.

"Right!" muttered Rivet and looked at his boots.

"Yeah. Right," said Scanner. They shuffled about and wouldn't look at me.

"So? What's the problem?" I asked casually, as if I'd be

able to fix whatever "the problem" was just by wiggling a finger or something.

"We dunno," Rivet replied. "We were running through fuel checks, control circuits, all the usual stuff, and then suddenly ... no power anywhere."

As soon as I heard that, I knew immediately what was wrong. Oh boy, the relief!

"D'you want to sit down a minute?" asked Scanner. "You look a bit funny."

My knees had melted so I let her steer me to the pilot's seat. "Sorry –" I said, and pointed vaguely to my face, which actually wasn't hurting at all any more – "it's the bruises."

Scanner scowled, her little red face a mass of folds.

"We don't like it, you know, what Hasp does. Beating people up and all."

Rivet glanced around like he was waiting for a bullet to pass his ear.

"Shudd*up,* Scanner," he hissed.

"I don't care! You all right now?"

I nodded. I was much more than all right. I felt Fortay was right there in the cockpit with me, and I knew what he'd done to cut the power of the *Uccello*. I could fix it, keep Hasp off my back, and maybe buy enough time to think of a "plan". "I'll need a small adjustable star wrench and a wire cutter," I said. "I know exactly what's wrong."

*   *   *

Crawling about behind the cockpit panel, I came up with a kind of plan. I would play along with Hasp's deception, pretend I was going to "take them all Home". I'd make myself look like the first Supa recruit to the Rebel cause and get them on my side. That way I'd be ready to pounce on whoever had set up me and Fortay. And I'd get control of my *Uccello*. By the time I crawled out, to find Sacks standing over me, I'd just about convinced myself that it was possible. But when I saw her, I remembered Hasp's promise: *Mess up and your little friend Sacks will get a bullet too.* My plan would be risking her life too.

"Hi," I said. I was glad she was alive but not glad that I was somehow responsible for her continuing to be so.

"Hi," she replied.

Hasp had roughed her up, and she looked as uncertain as I felt. But there was no time for thinking. I had to look cool, confident and convincing. I told them about the circuit breaker. Pretty simple stuff, but they seemed impressed. Then I said, "Hasp needs to know about this."

Rivet and Scanner looked at each other. They didn't seem keen.

"In fact I think everyone needs to know about this," I added. "I mean it's important – for getting Home, right?"

"Yeah." Rivet came round to the idea. "Yeah, you're right. I'll spread the word. Get everyone down 'ere..."

"Good," said Scanner. "We won't have to have that creep

Hasp down 'ere on 'is own!"

"Scanner ... stop it!" Rivet moaned, and disappeared.

By the time the whole settlement, including Hasp and his thugs, had gathered, it was dark. They stood in the pool of light by the *Uccello*'s door. Good, I thought, the more witnesses the better. All I had to do now was perform.

Hasp wasn't happy. I guessed he didn't like spectators that he hadn't invited. I knew I had to be very careful. If I said anything to spoil the story he'd thrown to the Rebels, he'd kill me. What I had to do was keep his lie alive, but take control of it. I sat at the top of the ramp steps and leant on the hull of the *Uccello*; my bird, my territory, my home.

"I've got something to show you all," I began and held up the innocent-looking little grey box of circuitry I'd disconnected from the guts of the *Uccello*. "This is what my brother, Fortay Nabisco, attached to the inside of the instrument panel. It was set to send a huge electromagnetic pulse that would deaden every power system on the craft. Which is just what it did. But it's also a detonator." Behind me, Rivet dropped a wrench and cursed quietly under his breath. There was the unmistakable sound of weapons being cocked ready to fire.

"You threatenin' us?" Hasp said in a monotone my father would have been proud of.

"No, not at all. I'm just informing you. Fortay was in a hurry. He didn't set it up properly. If he had, this ship would have spread in little pieces all over the prairie."

Still Hasp stayed cool. Not a twitch of a muscle anywhere. All he did was narrow his eyes, as if he were concentrating some sort of ray coming out of them and training it on my face. "Why're you tellin' us this?" he asked.

"Because when I found it, I could have detonated it. But I didn't."

"Course you didn't." Hasp allowed himself a shrug, and a little look around at his people. "You didn't want to die!" There was a general murmuring of agreement.

"My chances of surviving in your hands are pretty slim anyway, I think, once you get to my family's spacecraft." That actually made him smile, and raised a few nods of approval in the crowd. "I'll find the explosive that's still somewhere on this craft. I'll find it, no matter where Fortay hid it. I want to prove I'm on your side. I'll take you to the spacecraft. Willingly, not at gun point." Hasp hadn't expected that. I watched as the brain cells clicked and whirred behind the pale forehead and the dead eyes. "And as soon as I find it, we can leave for the space rocket, and your journey Home. Just as you and I discussed, Hasp." Hasp shot me a look of pure hate; he knew as well as I did we'd had no 'discussions'.

"Why should we believe you?" somebody shouted from the back.

I held up the box again. "Because I told you about this. Because I'll find that explosive. And because of this..." I knew the thugs could shoot to kill, so I pulled Fortay's gun out of my shirt by the barrel to make it obvious I wasn't about to point it at anyone. Then I put the butt in Hasp's hand and I breathed as slowly as I could manage. "Check it," I said. "It's loaded. I found it when I found the detonator. Fortay must have put it down there. I could have killed everyone in the cockpit and taken off. There would have been nothing you or your guards could have done to prevent it. But I didn't."

The crowd murmured. I could feel their approval, their belief in what I'd said. Now there wasn't a thing Hasp could do to me without blowing his own plans. He smiled for the crowd mirthful as a skull, and said, real quiet so only I could hear, "Find the explosive in twenty-four hours or you're dead." But it was just muscle flexing. I was taking control of the hook and the bait, and he knew it!

The crowd parted and Hasp disappeared into the night, leaving four extra guards at the door of the *Uccello*.

I stood up shakily and went inside the craft. The first part of my plan had worked and all I felt was a little nauseous. Scanner and Rivet stood with their mouths open in the loading area.

"Let's get to it," I said. "We got to search every inch. You guys take the tail section and the hold. I'll show Sacks where to look on the wings."

"Right," Scanner and Rivet said together, and disappeared, kind of dazed-looking, I thought.

As soon as they were out of earshot, Sacks hissed out of the dimness behind the panelling on the port wing. "What was that crap?" She had a way of making her face blank and angry at the same time, and she was doing it now.

"What do you mean?"

"If you really want to be on the Rebels' side, why can't you just tell the truth?"

"And what truth is that then?"

"You know what I mean."

I was suddenly very tired and my heart was still almost coming out of my mouth. I wanted to yell at her that I was scared. I wanted to yell at her to shut up. But I didn't do either. "Look, Sacks," I said. "I just want to get out of this alive, so be quiet and help me find the explosive."

I think the logic must have appealed to her because she did shut up and she began looking. She did a good job too. She called me to look at a spot under the inner lining of the starboard wing.

"What's that?" she asked, pointing up at the panelling.

"Just a bit of panelling."

"No! *That*."

I studied it again. There was a thumbprint in the corner of one of the panels. Clear, but faint.

"How did you notice that?"

Sacks shrugged. "Didn't feel right in here. So I just looked."

"I'd never have seen that," I reflected. I was impressed, but Sacks didn't want to care about my opinion. She swallowed her smile, looked at her boots and growled, "You going to look at it or what then?"

Up close I recognized the print. It was Fortay's: his left thumb, with the scar right down the middle. It seemed crazy that a smear of sweat from his thumb could still exist when he didn't. I pushed the edge of the panel and it dropped out of place. And there was the explosive, smoothed flat in a thin layer so that it looked like a patch.

"Will it blow up?" asked Sacks.

"I hope not!"

I took a nice slow breath and got to work. You never know with somebody else's work, what they might have done. Even your brother. I'd removed the main detonator system, but there might be a backup; something clever, something extra. But it seemed straightforward. The wires were tucked into the seam, where the membrane met the frame. There was nothing else. Fortay just hadn't had time. I cut the wires and peeled the explosive away from the panel. "That's it," I said. "We're all done here."

Sacks let out a big breath, too relieved not to smile. "How d'you know what to do?"

"Explosives, guns, they're my thing. My job. Sort of."

"Useful."

"Yeah, especially as we're on the same side now." I teased back, but she just growled, "I'm not on anyone's side. Only my own."

* * *

Just like I thought he would, Hasp pushed his narrow, rigid body into the space under the wing, to see the whole thing for himself. I put the peeled explosive in his hands, like dried skin. I told him we'd do final checks in daylight and then be ready to go. He didn't say much to that. I guess he was thinking as hard as I was about the next move. Whoever he had lined up to pull the string was going to have to be ready early. When he left, he took almost all the guards with him except two, to keep an eye on me and Sacks, and take us all back to the settlement.

We closed down everything on the *Uccello* and got ready to go. Standing in the light outside the craft door, Rivet cleared his throat, like he was about to make a big speech, and stepped in front of me with his arms crossed. "I weren't sure, you know, about that spacecraft stuff," he said. "What with you being a Supa and all. I mean, it all sounded nice —"

"Nice! *Nice!*" Scanner laughed at him. "Yeah, I should think it is *nice* to be goin' to the planet that's our *real* Home, where we *belong*!" She pulled the hood of his overalls over his eyes.

"Scanner, wait. I'm trying to *say* something 'ere!" He pushed her off, and stared me full in the face. "I wanna say something about Nero. I wasn't sure about you, Nero, but after the detonator and the explosive and all that... Well, Nero, I'm sure now."

The torchlight was hard and white, and Rivet's features cast deep shadows over his face. I tried to concentrate on the sorts of details that Father would have pointed out: the snub nose, the eyes set too close together. Father's voice came up into my head... *Never imagine that they are even worthy of a name. They are to you as one, simply Worker.* But that shy smile of Rivet's kept my attention. I'd never been given a smile like that before. A smile that you could see clear to the bottom of.

As we started to walk, Scanner's little red hand slapped my back. "Well, *I* was sure," she declared, "right from when you came in 'ere. I *knew.*"

Never imagine that they are even worthy of a name. They are to you as one, simply Worker. Never imagine that they are even worthy of a— Shut up, Dad! I warned. *Not right now.*

"You're one of us now," Scanner said to me, "You're all right."

No one had ever told me I was "all right" before. "That's very kind of you," I replied to Scanner and Rivet, adding, "I hope you get Home, like we all want." I felt bad that I was lying to them, and was glad that the torchlight didn't show me Sacks' face.

I'd been moved about with my head covered for the whole time I'd been with the Rebels. I'd heard them, spoken to them, seen a little of the inside of their tents – or at least Hasp's "quarters" – but I hadn't seen the whole settlement. I'd imagined something a little scruffy, like the dumps of plastic sheeting and corrugated steel the street fighters make. At night I'd thought there might be a few little pools of light from some kind of pathetic solar batteries or something. All in all, I was ready to be contemptuous enough to think, *Well, yeah, they are Workers, after all, and without us what can they do?*

So when we got to the top of the hill, I was dazzled at the sight of the settlement below. It was dotted with light; blue-white solar lights and red eyes of fire. It looked compact and organized; better in fact than most parts of the City looked. There were no nasty huts made of rubbish. All the homes were tall cones, with light and smoke trailing from the holes in their tops, like breath. It was amazing, and also weirdly familiar. Like the buffalo, it was something out of my dreams, like the little cone-shaped house my old guy had danced in front of!

"You OK, Nero?" Scanner touched my arm. I realized I'd been standing still and staring, probably for quite a while.

"He hasn't seen the settlement before," explained Sacks. "They been movin' him round with a bag on his head."

"Yeah," I breathed, just about getting my voice back. "It's ... amazing! What d'you call those ... huts?"

"Tents." Scanner shrugged. "Just tents."

"Can we get on now? I gotta get a Meal fix."

"Sorry, Rivet," said Scanner. "I forgot!"

Outside the biggest tent a huge guy with a tower of black hair was handing out food. My stomach, which had been empty for a long long time, recognized it as food even when

I didn't. There were no pink hot dogs, or scampies, no fry-shapes. There was just combi food: the green goop containing all you *need* to eat that gets made into all the different kinds of good stuff you might *want* to eat. I wondered how they'd got it. Then I remembered a big delivery-craft crash a while back. Father had been quite pleased. It knocked a hole in the MacDonald family power base, he said. Word never got round that Rebels had seized the cargo. There was another smaller pot of goop that looked like the Meal that ended up in foil packets. They'd taken a whole delivery of it from the *Uccello*.

We joined the Rebels waiting for food, and I noticed that only a few still needed Meals too. Out of maybe thirty Rebels there were only five Product addicts. Father would have been very disappointed.

The ground between the tents was beaten flat and bare, and the solar lights cast a hazy glow. In some of the shadows, where the pools of light didn't quite overlap, Hasp had stationed his thugs. They all looked the same: big solid figures with black flak jackets and helmets and three kinds of gun. They were just like the guys my father used. I counted eight of them, just standing, apparently doing nothing. Low-key, but nice and menacing. The sort of protection a Supa family head would have, when he knew he wasn't everybody's favourite guy. So there was no way I could get up and tell everyone that Hasp was a fraud and we'd all better jump aboard the *Uccello* without him.

All the Rebels cared about right now was food. They stood in line watching the man with the high-rise hair splatting combi onto plastic platters. They were all men, or looked like it, most of them in their twenties and thirties. There were a few whiskery old-timers among them, and only a handful as young as us four. All were dressed in some version of Station standard, but the bright overalls had got discoloured with time and had been patched or mended with other materials. Some of the younger guys had coloured wires braided into hair they wore long and wild, and some wore fine strips of wrapping wound tightly round their heads. A couple had bits of Supas' blacks – drainpipes and a sleeveless flak jacket. Had they taken Fortay's clothes from his body? I didn't want to think about it.

There was no furniture in the big tent, just the ground and a few bits of floor covering that looked as if they'd come from a Station somewhere. The four of us took our plates of green porridge and sat down in a pool of solar light. It wasn't the greatest Meal ever, but I didn't remember ever being so hungry, so I didn't look up until Scanner nudged me. "Look!" she said. "Look!"

Every face was turned my way, open and trusting. The Rebels kept on looking, until all I could do was sit and take the quiet, smiling gazes of all those people falling on me like searchlights. At last I managed a kind of feeble, "Hi."

A few of them nodded back uncertainly, as if words were a new idea that they might try out sometime. Then one old guy, with a strand of pink wrapping around his head, spoke up. "You're that Supa, in't you? The Supa who's takin' us Home."

Takin' us home?! He made me sound like I was putting the whole lot of them in my car and taking them to my house for dinner.

"An' tha's the girl you saved, innit?" said a younger man with green wire in his yellow hair, nodding his head towards Sacks and her plate of food.

"Well," I said, "yeah. But she kind of saved me…"

The old man got up and walked towards me. I got up too, not sure what was going to happen. He took my right hand in his and waggled it up and down. "This 'ere's what we used to do in the old days. Shake an' say our names. Cable's my name. I'm shakin' your hand now and I'm sayin' my thanks. We'll all be goin' where we should be 'cos of you."

He let go of my hand and stumped away into the night. I watched him until he'd disappeared between the tents. When I turned round, all the other Rebels were standing with their hands out towards me. One by one they came and shook my right hand, and as they did so, each one said their name. Even the guy with the food put his ladle down and came up to me. "Grubber," he announced in a voice like an engine revving, and my hand disappeared into a great dark hole at the centre of his fist.

Last of all came Scanner and Rivet. Rivet nearly crushed my

fingers in his big bony palm. "Rivet. That's me," he said, "in case you'd forgotten after all the other names!"

Scanner slid her narrow hand into mine. "Well, you know my name," she said. "But I'll change it, I think, when I gets to Home." The smile she gave me could have lit up a whole block of the City.

Sacks just hung back and watched everyone else. I made sure I didn't look at her, not even once.

"You better come along with us," said Rivet. "You in't got y'own tent, so Hasp says you gotta stay in ours." He pointed to the two thug-minders, waiting at the edge of the group.

"Right. Well, thanks."

"Yeah," said Sacks finally. "Thanks."

As we left the conversation welled up behind us. I thought of what the old guy had said – *The Supa who's takin' us Home!* – and felt as if I'd swallowed a ton of lead along with the green goop.

sacks

THERE wasn't much to Scanner and Rivet's tent inside: carpet bits and scraps laid down over dried grass; two piles of packing material – bubble wrap, plastic foil and that – to make beds; a little fire in the middle; an old tin can, black on the outside; and a big plastic water bottle. But it felt nice. As soon as I was in there I wanted to lie down and sleep, as if it were my platform at the Station.

"Boots off!" ordered Rivet. "Gotta keep the floor dry."

"I'll make a drink," said Scanner, and she poured water into the tin, threw a few bits of green in with it, and set it on the fire. Rivet pulled the piles of bedding round, and we all four sat down on it. The little flames came up and sent orange pictures over the walls. Scanner poured hot water and green bits into another tin, and passed it round so we could all take a drink.

On the Station, when work was done, I had Meals and TV. When we worked, Mott talked and I listened, or not. But during down time he kept to his end, mostly, and I kept to mine. If we ever had Workers to check the auto systems, they came with Supas to watch them, so all we did was stand around and talk about circuits or delivery days while they waited for their transport. But this sitting for no reason, with no TV going on and no one to watch? Never.

The tin came to me and I sipped from it. The liquid was hot and sharp, and it caught at my throat as it went down, but I didn't care. I passed the tin on to Rivet. "We could be drinking from a bowl on Home before too long!" he exclaimed excitedly.

Scanner took the tin from him. "Yes!" she said. "Won't have to use some old leaves that might be toxic there. We'll be able to pick our food from all around us!"

Nero took the bowl. "Yes," he agreed, "that's it!"

He spoke softly and just stared in the fire. At least he wasn't getting much pleasure out of his lies. Why didn't anyone else see that something about his talk wasn't right? I wanted Scanner and Rivet to feel it, but they were too busy dreaming of Home and how it would be there.

I didn't want to hear about Home any more. Home wasn't real. This was real, the tent and the leaping light, and the faces round the fire. Why wasn't this enough for Rivet and Scanner – for them all? The memory of a fire and faces, of a woman brushing my cheek with a feather, came up again. I reached inside my clothes, where I still had my two feathers hidden. "Look," I said, "'tis two feathers."

"What?" said Scanner.

"Feathers. Off an Alien I seen with Mott. A flyin' one. Their skins is made of thousands of feathers, all together, so they look smooth." I held the feathers out for Scanner to see but she held back. "They isn't toxic or nothin'?" she asked.

"What are you like, Scanner?" Rivet shook his head. "Outside isn't *all* toxic. If it was as toxic as TV said, we'd be dead by now!" They both laughed.

Scanner took the feathers to hold, one in each hand. In turn she held them close to her eyes. "Good design, innit?"

"We get Aliens flying over the camp sometimes," said Rivet. "First time I saw 'em I was so scared, I thought my legs might snap with shaking!"

"If Aliens was dangerous, like TV said..." Scanner waggled the feathers in front of Rivet.

"Get off, Scanner. Makes sense to me that Aliens isn't safe even if they isn't toxic. This isn't our planet, remember! Anyway, I've seen 'em lots of times. Little brown ones and big white ones – skinny, long legs. Out on the prairie."

"Cranes," Nero said quietly. "The big white ones are called cranes."

"Who calls 'em cranes?" I asked him.

"Oh, I dunno. Maybe the first Supas who came here from Home. You know, like five hundred years ago or something. It's just a name. I learnt it when I was a kid." He shrugged and took another drink from the tin.

"Where? Where'd you learn it?"

"Oh, I don't remember."

He shrugged some more, and started finding the fire really interesting. But I wouldn't leave it be. "What were those other Aliens we saw called, Nero, the big ones with four legs?"

"Um ... I don't remember."

"Funny you don't. Because I thought it was the only true thing you've ever said!"

There was a very big silence. Rivet and Scanner were sitting there, stabbing me with their eyes, but Nero wouldn't look up. "Who cares, anyway?" he said. "They're Aliens, right, and we aren't staying on this *Alien* planet!" They all three laughed, and the feathers twirled out of Scanner's fingers and fell towards the fire. I leapt up to save them and knocked Nero over, making the drink spill on the bedding. They all stopped laughing and stared at me.

I was fired up then. Everything that had happened since the Station burned had flown into the air and landed in a pattern that I began to make out for the first time. "They're important, these feathers." I held one in each hand. "And there's somethin' you ought to know about them. This one's from an Alien – that *crane*. And this one here was growin' out of the side of a Unit. *A Unit*, right, from *Planet Home*. How come what's on Home, up there in the sky, has got feathers same as Aliens? How come cranes has got blood that's red, like ours? How come the Supas has been lying about *everything* but *not* about Home?"

Scanner jumped up and Rivet beside her. "What are you

sayin'?" She shoved me hard. For something so small, she could hit! "You're a freak," she said, and shouted at my face, "You don't even *want* to get Home!"

"I heard you was a spy," added Rivet. "You told the Supas about the raid on Station 27."

"Yeah, and that's likely true, isn't it? Because my Mott, all I'd ever known, got killed by your Hasp!"

Rivet pushed me and I fell down with the two of them standing over me, ready to give me a good kicking, I thought.

"Let's just calm down, everybody." Nero stepped between Rivet and Scanner. He was smaller than either me or Rivet, and thin, but right then he looked older than any of us. In the half-light of the fire he could've been Hasp's age, or even Mott's. "We're all tired, right? Sacks has had one beating since she got here. She doesn't need another. Let's just get some sleep."

Rivet gave me the wet bedding to sleep on, and the place furthest from the fire. But it didn't matter; the good feeling inside the tent had gone, and there was too much in my head to sleep. I lay still, with my face to the wall, watching until the shadows stopped moving and all the others were breathing deeply and evenly. Slowly, really slowly, I got up and crawled out through the door flap.

The solar lights were dimmed down to save power, and the tent door was in shadow. I looked round. The thugs had gone, and there was no sign of any other of Hasp's men any-where. I crawled round the tent wall, keeping out of the light until I got to the back. Beyond the next tent, the darkness of the prairie started where the grey glow from the solar lamps ended. That's what I wanted, that dark space away from people and things. I didn't need to have Home at the other side; the space was enough.

I was afraid, but I made myself walk past the last tent; running, even in bare feet, would have made too much noise. But when I reached the dark, I ran, even though I couldn't see where I was going. I could feel the cold, moist strands of the grass under my soles, and smell its green scent. I ran faster and faster, stumbling onto my hands and knees as I went up the slope and then down the other side, until all I could see was dark: the dark of the prairie, black under my feet, and the dark of the sky, black with cloud.

I lay down in the grass, cold and shivering, but calm now, clearer in my head. I could feel the Earth, with me stuck on it turning with its armour of cloud, and I could feel Mott's voice inside me: *Go! Get Outside. There's your home. Outside! There's your home!*

Maybe I should slip away in the darkness now, I thought. And when Nero and Rivet and Scanner and all of them had gone off chasing whatever it was they were all really chasing, I could come back and live alone in a tent, on the big green prairie, with the cranes and the buffalo.

I looked out into the dark for so long, I started to see things. Or so I thought, when I first noticed the faintest of little glows, far off over the black prairie. It moved, and the way it moved I knew what it was, like I knew the shiver in a batch of Units or the wheeze of Mott's breath. It was a Supa aero-craft, moving slowly on low, low lights. It was close to the ground, searching for something, coming towards the settlement. I would have got up to run, but Nero's hand clamped over my mouth. I waited a moment, for him to think I was still, then I bit him. Hard.

"Ow! I might have been ready to slit your throat," he said. "I mean, I am a Supa and so *very untrustworthy*."

"Shuddup, Nero."

"I'll shut up when you tell me what you're doing up here. Waiting to signal to an enemy craft?"

"What with? Search me! Go on, do it!"

"No! No. OK. I believe you."

"That's more than I do you then. Enemy craft! They ain't *your* enemy."

"They're *everybody's* enemy right now! Everybody's, that is, except Hasp and his men, who seem to have mysteriously disappeared. When that craft gets here, they won't wait to look at ID cards."

"You think I don't know that!"

We both got up and began running the same way, back towards the settlement. I could have run away, out onto the prairie, to wait for it all to be over. But I didn't. Nero could have run for the *Uccello* and just flown away. We'd both chosen to take the same side.

We got as far as the bottom of the last slope, before the settlement, when a flash lit up the ridge above us. A huge flare hung in the sky, then the hit of an explosion went through the hillside like a shudder, a great fist hitting the ground. Without knowing how I got there, I found I was lying on the path, with Nero at my side. "It must have come round the other side of the hill, while we we running here." His voice was quiet and shaking.

There was another flare, and shouts and screams came over the hill from the settlement. I wondered how many Rebels had been killed already. Not all, for sure, because a moment later some of them came crawling out of the grass, breathless and coughing, but alive! Scanner, Rivet, Grubber, Flame and a couple of others I didn't know.

"They came out of nowhere," said Rivet. "First we heard was the roar of the craft, taking a low pass over the settlement!"

"They ain't shootin. They're using gas ... Rebels dropping unconscious where they stand..." added Grubber. "They'll put them back on Stations." He sounded ready to cry.

"Hasp's gone!" Flame wailed.

"We've got to go back," urged Scanner, "gather people up. Get them on the Uccello."

"We can't, Scanner," said one of the Rebels I didn't know. "We'll be gassed too!"

"Bead's right," said Rivet. "We can't do any good that way!"

Nero's voice came out of the dark, still trembling, but determined sounding. "Here's what we'll do. Get to the *Uccello* and take off, fast. As soon as they see us, they'll follow, and that'll give anyone still conscious on the ground a chance at least. But we've got to move fast."

Everyone was frightened and sweating by the time we'd run up the loading ramp and onto the *Uccello*. We couldn't risk any light until the moment we took off, so in the hold we were still in total darkness. The Rebels murmured and cursed and called out softly in the dark, checking to see if we'd all made it aboard. There were eight of us all together; eight out of close on thirty from the settlement.

Nero sat in the pilot's seat and immediately seemed to grow bigger. The shake had gone out of his voice; he wasn't scared any more. Scanner was in the co-pilot's seat, and Rivet and I squeezed in either side. The argument over the feathers and Planet Home didn't seem to matter now: We had to get the *Uccello* into the air. Nero flicked switches with Scanner. Rivet and I shoved the circuit units back into their slots under the cockpit panel. Out of the window we could see blossoms of red light burst on the clouds above us. Rivet cursed.

"They'll all be caught!" Scanner wailed.

"If you got away, other people did too," Nero assured her. "Let's get this craft up there so they get a chance. Scanner? Ready?"

"Yep."

"Rivet?"

"I haven't checked all the landing circuits."

"No time. We don't need 'em for take-off. Scanner! What about the runway? I don't want to use all our power on a vertical take-off."

"Take her round ninety degrees. It's right there."

"But it's got a load of grass and stuff all over to hide it." said Rivet.

"She's pretty robust," said Nero. "We'll just have to go for it."

The craft shivered alive and moved to point at the runway. "We need lights for this, so our cover is about to blow," Nero told us, then turned to look at me. "Your first flight, huh?" He grinned. "Hold on!"

The *Uccello*'s headlights illuminated the runway. It didn't look like much to me; just a flat bit of grass. The engines shouted so loud, I thought we would all explode, and then Nero was off. Bits of grass whirled past the window as the *Uccello* shed her camouflage covering .

I'd watched take-offs before, a thousand times. I'd seen craft racing from the Station and off into the sky, but I'd never thought how it would feel to be inside one. Everything shook. There were fast, deep shakes that came up my legs and made my eyes move in their sockets. There were bigger shakes that made the instruments rattle and the tools in the box on the floor chatter. And there were huge shakes that made the whole cockpit move, so that at any moment you felt your feet might go through the floor to thin air. I couldn't see how she could shake so much and not fall into a heap of metal and screws.

Through the cockpit bubble I could see the ground racing underneath us, as if it were being pulled from behind. To our left, the line of the hill blurred with our speed. We could see the lights of the Supa craft making passes over the settlement. It was something like the *Mandraya* with a thick body and stumpy wings, slow-looking. It didn't notice us at first – it was too busy seeing all the destruction it was causing down below. Then its lights spilled over the rim of the hill and began to head towards us.

The shaking and rattling got worse; my brains would surely work loose and run out of my ears. The ragged runway went faster and faster beneath us, pulling us away from the enemy craft. But their lights moved like a smooth white star, closer and closer. We could see the cockpit of the craft now, and the metal shine of its unmarked side. Time stretched like rubber. Closer the lights came, louder shook the *Uccello*. Closer, louder, closer, louder – like a contest to see who could make the world burst with noise.

And then, silence. The shaking stopped, and time snapped back to normal speed. We were up and moving as if there were no effort to it at all, with no sound but a sort of hissing as the air slithered over the *Uccello*'s skin.

Nero took us high, so straight that all we could see was cloudy sky. He and Scanner were pressed in their seats, and Rivet and I hung on where we could, with the cockpit almost vertical. We popped out through the cloud under an arc of stars, and levelled our flight. The moon was like the rim of a pale cup and down below was a fluffy plain of silver-blue, going on for ever.

There wasn't time to look. Dots and streaks of red streamed past the window and faded into the air. Scanner cried out, "They're onto us!"

"You didn't say they'd got weapons!" said Rivet.

"You didn't ask!" Nero snapped back. "It's just a little automatic fire. They won't hit us. We can outrun a tub like that!"

The *Uccello* dropped. I thought we'd been hit, but when I looked at Nero he was smiling. He turned the craft so fast that the moon seemed to flip away, and the sky seemed to change to another set of stars and a paler horizon. Above us and ahead was the Supas' craft. Nero took us right underneath it, before its heavy body could turn to follow. A moment later the stars were gone and we were down in the cloud, with wisps of it racing past outside, like material being torn to shreds. "I'll give them another sight of us in a minute," he said. "Get them to burn a little more fuel. There's no refuelling out here any more, not now Station 27's gone – 98 doesn't keep any. They'll have to head back soon."

Nero turned us again and the shreds of cloud scattered

past for minutes more. Then the *Uccello* headed up above the cloud and climbed in a long spiral. We looked out of the cockpit bubble, watching for a sign of the Supas' lumpy craft; a line of red and a rattle of bullets scraping the *Uccello*'s back told us where it was. "Whoops … on our tail. Hold on."

We swooped straight up again, but this time the *Uccello* didn't seem so light. There was a screaming sound from the starboard wing. Even Scanner's bright face went pale.

"They hit us…" she breathed.

"That engine don't sound too good, Nero," said Rivet.

Trails of red were on both sides of us now, shooting up from the craft, getting closer. Nero just looked ahead into the sky, which was starting to brighten at the edge. His mouth was a straight line and his eyes had almost disappeared in narrow cracks. "Nobody hits my bird," he declared. "Nobody." The *Uccello* dropped again. This time I was sure it wasn't meant to happen, but it levelled. Then it turned very sharply so that above us, and in front, was the Supa craft. We were heading right for it.

"What are you doing?" Rivet was yelling. He looked ready to push Nero off his seat.

"Shut up!" was all Nero said.

The fat craft filled the cockpit view. Rivet and Scanner put their hands over their eyes, but I couldn't stop looking; stuck, as if in a nightmare. The lights on their wing; the line of bullets from their nose; a face in their cockpit. Tight with fear and anger that face was, frozen in a piece of time. It was too small to name and yet I knew it: Hasp.

Then all of us, even Nero, screamed. But Nero's scream meant something different. It meant "I've won." And he had. The sky in front of us was clear, with nothing in it but the orange beginnings of the day. Far below, and to our left, the big craft was falling, twisting in the air, trying to pull out of the dive Nero had forced it to make. "Only way to lose them," he explained. "With that engine malfunctioning, we didn't have the speed to out-climb them. Sorry I scared you." Nobody said anything.

After a while Rivet cleared his throat and started taking readings off the little dials on the instrument panel. Scanner began to fidget too, flicking switches on and off. "We got to go back, Nero," she said, "and pick up survivors. You got to turn round."

"I can't turn round, Scanner. If I go back, we'll be stuck. I won't have enough fuel to fly to the next dump. The next Supa craft will just pick us all off."

"But we can't go Home without them," Rivet insisted.

"We can't go back. We have three hours' more flying time. It's three hours to the nearest fuel dump, and four to the City. We'll talk when we get to the dump."

There was no argument; Rivet and Scanner could read the fuel gauges, just as Nero could, so Rivet went into the hold to tell the others. I leaned on the wall and wondered what was inside Nero's head. Nero didn't need a co-pilot for level flying, leaving Scanner free to go with Rivet to the hold, to rest. I sat in the co-pilot's seat, and kicked the cockpit door closed for a bit of quiet. "Where are we going, Nero?" I asked.

He stared ahead, or checked lights and dials – anything but look at me. "I told you. A fuel dump."

"And then where are we going?"

"Home. I keep telling you..."

"All right, Nero. Where are we *really* going?"

He took a while to answer, and then whispered, "The fuel dump first. I don't really know. Maybe I could fly you guys back to the settlement, then take the *Uccello* back to the City. I don't know, Sacks. My plans haven't worked out so well."

"What plans?"

"My playing-along-with-Hasp plans. Hasp killed my brother, but I'm sure he was working for someone – not a Rebel. The *Uccello* and all that Home rocket stuff – it was just bait. A bait to get a lot of Rebels aboard and then take them … to somewhere … for someone." He shrugged. "I wanted to find out who that was..."

"So you lied to all those people, just for a bit of revenge."

"If I'd tried the truth, d'you think they'd have believed it? Do you think Hasp wouldn't have killed me and betrayed them just the same?"

I knew he was right. Nobody seemed to want to give up on the dream of Home. "So whose side are you on now then?" I persisted.

"Like you, Sacks, on my own side. I just want to find out

who was behind my brother's death."

We sat, letting the sun flood our faces, not speaking for a while. "Hasp was on that craft," I said eventually, "I'm sure I saw him."

"Yeah, I saw him too," replied Nero. "I don't understand any of this, Sacks, and I thought I did." Nero slumped in his chair and rubbed one hand over his hair. "I thought I'd been really clever, and kind of hooked him. But I think I just spooked him into getting his friends to destroy the settlement."

"Did he ask you stuff about your real name?"

"Yeah, he did! And yours too. I don't get it, why?"

We sat still again, trapped in another thicket of tangles. I probed Nero more gently this time. "What *are* you going to do, Nero?"

"I don't know..."

"Tell them they aren't going Home. It's only fair."

"You tell 'em."

"They don't trust me, Nero."

He sighed, shrugged, scratched his head, and at last replied, "OK, OK. I'll do it. Just not yet. It's keeping them going. They want to go Home so badly!"

Then the cockpit door opened and Rivet stepped in, yawning. He looked from Nero to me and back. "I was thinking," he said. "I never checked them landing circuits. I should do now. In case there's some problem."

Nero cleared his throat and spoke up, strong and steady.

"Yeah, good idea, Rivet. Sacks'll help. She knows a bit about circuits."

I wasn't ready to speak after my talk with Nero, so I just shut up and got on with the circuits as best I could. By the time Rivet and I were nearly done, the sun was shining so brightly, I almost didn't see the little trail of silver solder on the last circuit. "What's this, Rivet?" I asked.

He leant across, looked and cursed. "There's a bypass on this circuit, Nero."

"What?!" Nero snapped his eyes from the sky.

"There! Look!"

Nero reached over and ran his bony fingers around the board, squinting at the Supas' writing on the back. Then he cursed too, so badly Mott would have been proud. "That's the landing-gear lowering control" he said. "Another of my brother's little surprises. He's booby-trapped something. I'd guess that as soon as we try and lower the landing gear, it'll connect to..."

Scanner, standing at the cockpit door, shut it behind her.

"No point scaring anybody who don't need scaring," she said.

"Right. Well, I'd say, knowing Fortay, another stash of plastic explosive?"

Scanner rubbed her crinkled scalp with both hands. "But we landed once already. I mean, since we took this craft..."

"Yeah," said Rivet. "If something bad was going to happen, it would have happened then…" But he didn't sound like he believed it.

"Maybe," Nero reflected. "But I taught my brother a lot about explosives, about all the little tricks you can pull with detonators. He rigged the first stash so it would blow not on the first take-off but on the second. I think he could have done the same with the landing gear."

"Why do that?" asked Rivet.

"He was working in a hurry. Before I got to the hangar on the morning of the raid, right?" Nero sounded scared. It was weird how he changed from tough to frightened so fast. His voice sank into a shaky whisper, like he was talking to himself. "Fortay got to the hangar that morning. He wasn't sure something bad was going to happen. He just suspected. He knew we might have to take off from the Station in a hurry, and head for home. There was no time to de-rig the explosives he'd put in before, so he'd set them to go off on the second take-off or, failing that, on the second landing. If we'd got away safely, he could have disconnected the lot when we got back. If we hadn't, then whoever took the *Uccello* was in trouble."

There was a big silence. It was pretty clear Nero was on the right track. I could see it, even without being Fortay's relative. But Rivet didn't want it to be true.

"We looked everywhere!" he said. "There's nowhere explosives could be."

As soon as he said it, we all thought the same thing, but

only Scanner spoke up. "We looked everywhere *inside*. Maybe not everywhere *outside*." She didn't look at Rivet, but she didn't need to – he was already riled up.

"I looked outside," he shouted. "I looked all over the wings and the tail. *Everywhere* outside."

"Not everywhere." Nero's voice was still quiet, but the shake was starting to go. "When the gear is down on the ground, the doors fold back against the underside into that little depression that's made to take them, right?"

Scanner and Rivet nodded, and I did too, though I had never noticed such a thing.

"So *that's* where he put it," Nero said. "Spread thin on the outside of the doors, or in that little dip where the doors fit. That's where I would've put it."

"Can't we just cut the wiring he did on the circuit?" I suggested.

"No, Sacks. Too risky. He might have thought of that. I mean, if he ever listened to what I told him, and it looks like he did—"

"Right then," I said, "I'm getting out there to scrape it off. Or whatever." I didn't really think about what I was saying. I just had a picture in my head of me hanging under the craft and peeling off the explosive, as easily as Nero had peeled it off the wing panel inside. And I wanted to do something, to prove to the Rebels I could be trusted; to show I was, after all, on their side.

Rivet and Scanner just stared with their mouths open, and Nero laughed. "D'you realize how fast this thing goes? No matter what we tie you on with, you go out of those cargo doors and you'll be wrapped round the tail fin in less than half a second!"

"Isn't there anything to hang on to?" I asked feebly.

"No." Rivet shook his head. "Not a thing."

"There could be something," said Scanner, 'if we put a cable between the forward service panel and the cargo door..." She looked at me and smiled.

"And how're we going to get a cable out of the service panel?" Rivet was getting excited again. "Don't be a durr, Scanner!"

"I'll tell you how, Rivet, *durr*." Scanner's little face was redder than ever, and she pushed her finger into Rivet's belly as she spoke. "I'm small enough to wriggle down there, from the back of the cockpit instrument panel. Then, if I drop it right, just right, the slipstream'll take it right along the middle of the plane to the cargo doors."

Rivet wasn't impressed. "And if it goes off one side and gets sucked into an engine... Then what?"

Scanner shoved Rivet against the wall. "Well, you got any better ideas? If you'd searched the outside proper, first off..."

Scanner and Rivet were leaning almost nose to nose over the co-pilot's seat. Nero's hand came up between them. "OK, everybody, OK," he said. "Like Scanner says, what better ideas do we have?"

Rivet looked at his feet and sniffed.

"Right," Nero continued, "this is the deal. We have an hour to the landing strip, and maybe seventy minutes' more fuel before we have to land. Either we get rid of the explosive now, or we risk landing with it and—"

"There's a hundred feet of cable in the hold," Scanner interrupted. "It's heavy. Sacks, you get Grubber to help you get it up here, OK?"

I could see the faces of the Rebels down in the hold, now that the light had come up down there. There were Grubber and Flame. I was glad she'd made it, even though she'd got me a beating from Hasp. There were two tall young men, Bead and Spadey, who looked strong and handy. Both had Grubber's dark hair and arms as hard as metal. Of all the settlement, we had only these. I hoped Nero's fancy flying had saved some of the rest from being sent back to rot on Product, working in Stations.

"We got a bit of a problem..." Rivet told them.

They took it pretty well. There wasn't much point in panicking, after all. They helped us get the coil of cable into the cockpit, just as Scanner's voice came up faintly from down under the cockpit floor... "It's a tight space down 'ere! You'll have to feed it down a bit at a time."

"That means we can't lob it all and hope the slipstream'll take it," added Rivet, almost pleased he'd been proved right.

Nero didn't look up from the control panel to speak.

"Look in the locker over the panel above my head," he said. "There's some fine nylon rope in there. It's ancient, but it's still good. Loop it over one end of the cable and throw that."

Of course! A guide rope, to pull the cable through! I nearly told him well done. Then I thought better of it. I shouted down to Scanner instead. "D'you hear that Scanner?"

"No need to shout," she replied. "I can hear all of you stompin' about up there!"

Rivet tied the rope to one end of the cable, then passed it and the first bit of cable through to Scanner. I looked down after it, and I could just see the flash of Scanner's torch between the panel back and the hull. It didn't look big enough for a crane's skinny leg to me, let alone a human! But we were nearly ready to try. Grubber and the two boys went aft, to get the cargo doors ready. As Rivet and I left the cockpit to get to the rear-cargo doors, Nero said, "I'll bring her speed down as low as I can, but we have thirty minutes before we're out of fuel and we'll have to land the quick way."

"Right, Nero." Rivet grinned. "No pressure, then!"

The doors were in a tight compartment beyond the main hold. We were all jammed in there, Rivet, Bead, Grubber, Spadey, Flame and me, as we pulled the doors open. Then we were crouched on hands and knees, facing each other over the hole of rushing air and the long drop to the ground.

"Now what?" said Bead.

"Yeah," added Spadey, "now what?"

"Thing is," said Rivet, his round face creasing almost as much as Scanner's, "we can't see where the rope's coming from 'ere."

"We'd need to sort of…"

"…dangle out."

We stared down at the wisps of cloud tearing past. I'd said I would go out on the cable once it was there, so it made sense for me to do the "dangling".

"I'll do it," said Flame quietly. "Let me!"

"No need for that, Flame," said Spadey. "You got nothing to make up for. Hasp's his own man."

"Anyway, Flame," I said. "I'm smaller. I'll be easier to hold."

"I'll tie your hair back for you," said Flame. "You don't want it in your eyes." She stepped behind me and bound my hair up with a bit of torn rag. "Good luck," she whispered.

I took Mott's pouch and handed it to Rivet. "Take this. Give it to Nero if I don't need it. Now," I said, "hold my legs." They all looked at me. "Do it!" I said. "We ain't got time to mess about." *Thirty minutes,* I thought. *Less now, probably. twenty-five, twenty-four…*

They took a couple of minutes to tie themselves on to the craft so they couldn't fall out, then Grubber and Rivet took one leg, and Bead and Spadey took the other. Flame held the edge of the doors down so they didn't trip anyone up.

"You got knees like sprockets!" said Bead.

"No," said Spadey, "worse than that. Never felt anything so knobbly!"

"Shuddup," I said. "*Shuddup!*"

They pushed my body out into the air, and upside down I hung from the bottom of the craft, beaten by the rushing air and the huge noise of the engines so that I felt slapped all over. Bits of white cloud whipped my face so fast, I felt my eyes were being turned on and off. *Twenty minutes, nineteen? Less ... less...*

I forced my eyes hard open and thought of my sight as a shot from a gun, going out straight and finding what it wanted. And there was Scanner! Upside down like me, her tiny red head and little hands sticking out of the forward service hatch! I waved and she waved back. Her smile flashed white in her red face and the rope fell towards me easily as a spanner dropped in a lift shaft. I saw my hand reach out... And then I was inside and Rivet and Spadey were pulling the rope hand over hand over hand, until it turned to hard metal cable, and the boys were all laughing and patting me on the back. We pulled it tight on the winch used to haul in heavy cargo. Everything was ready.

"Who's going out on this?" asked Spadey, looking like he hoped nobody was going to ask him.

"Me," Rivet and I said together.

"No," I insisted, "me. I'm doing it. Because you can't do without Rivet or these tough boys, but you can do without me."

Rivet didn't say any more. He made a harness of rope with a metal clip that could hook over the cable. Then he pulled a sort of backpack thing out of a locker. "It's a chute," he said. "It's supposed to stop you falling. Supas use 'em in crashes and that. Sort of keeps you up in the air. Don't exactly know how, but Supas sets store by 'em and they ain't keen on dyin' as a rule!"

"But I can't move with that on."

"Don't fight with me," said Rivet. "You put it on or I'll hold you in 'ere." He sounded just like Mott. There wasn't time to fight anyway.

I put a wrench, some wire cutters and a screwdriver in my overalls and stuck my legs out through the door so they hung in the air. My fingers bound like solder to the door frame, but I knew I had to let go. I said to myself, *Fifteen minutes ... fourteen...* But still my fingers were tight, kept there by the empty air and the long fall below. They were all looking at me now, crouched round the open door, waiting for me to keep my word. I thought of Mott talking through the wound in his chest, of the sucking mouth holes of the Units, of the colours lighting my platform, of all the days and nights I'd spent in a daze of Product. It was all gone, all in the past, like the strands of cloud falling behind the plane as we flew, rushing past this empty hole. And the empty hole was the future with nothing in it at all, until I put something there; and I had nothing to put in it but myself and no more time to do it than now. If I didn't let go of the door, the future would always be empty for sure, and that made me more afraid than the thought of falling.

So I loosed my fingers from the frame, and the cable and harness took me. They sagged so badly and the chute thing on my back pulled me down. I swung under the plane and concentrated on looking up at the metal panels of the hull. I could barely get my fingers under the cable to pull myself along. I hung there, with the metal biting my fingers and the dead weight on my shoulders, and wished and wished I was back on my platform, with a bellyful of Meal and half a ton of Product! Then my strength tightened and the future held its plain hand out to me again. *Ten minutes now,* I thought. *Just ten minutes...*

I was a long way from the landing gear doors. I reached above my head and held the cable. Reach. Pull. Reach. Pull. Each pull stripped skin from my fingers and scraped my rope harness against the twists of the metal. Pull. Pull. Pull. Still all I could see was the smooth silver surface, with its little pattern of screws and pot rivets, and a few scrapes of dirt.

The Supas' little black marks, their letters and words, told me I was near. They always made their marks on important things. One more pull, which made my hands slippery with blood, and I was there. The aft edge of the doors was in front of my nose, and to either side were the dips that took the doors when the plane was grounded. The light was all wrong, coming thinly through the clouds and falling so that the curve of the fuselage put the door dips into shadow. I stretched out to feel inside each one, but with the tight cable and ropes I couldn't reach.

Right then, Nero dropped and turned the *Uccello*, just a little, slowly and gently, almost as if he knew what I needed. The early sun flooded up from the horizon and splashed full into both of the dips! The right one shone clean, reflecting back the light, but the left was dull. Spread over it was a grey-blue layer, rolled thin and stuck down, with two tiny silver wires sneaking out. I'd found it! I only had to get my fingers under its edge and it would just peel away. My fingers itched with the thought, but Rivet's safe harness held me too tight! *Eight minutes, seven minutes. Less … less … always less…*

I felt for the knots in the harness. They were as stiff and hard as stones, and my hands were so cold, I felt the blood over them icing up. I pushed and worried at the one knot on my belly, pressing with my bleeding thumbs to make it go back through its loop. Suddenly it did, but the little slack I'd expected was a huge loosening, and I dropped, dangling by my legs, blown too hard by the wind to get back up close to the explosive. So I used the way the wind blew to make myself swing: backwards so I had nowhere to look but down – I shut my eyes; then forward, towards the silver of the plane and the little patch of killing blue-grey explosive. Each time I took a bigger swing, until I could grab the cable with one hand. And now with the other. I could reach the explosive.

Nero was taking the craft lower. I felt the tilt of her body and heard the changing tone of the engine. *Six minutes. Less ... less ... less...*

My nails curled under one edge, then the other, then the third. But instead of falling clear of the hull and the little silver detonator wires, the explosive sheet wrapped itself around the cable; the wires were longer than I'd thought. They'd pulled through their neat little holes and still reached it. It could still explode. *Four minutes*, I thought. *Four minutes. Less ... less ... less...*

There weren't any choices left. No time to pull forward to free the sheet from the cable. No time to fight with another of Rivet's good knots to reach and cut the little wires. There was only one thing to do: cut the cable. Its weight alone might not be enough to pull the wires and explosive free so the whole thing fell before it detonated. But with my weight added, it would work. I pulled out the wire cutters and waved them at Scanner's face – still poking from the forward hatch. "Cut the cable your end!" I yelled. I saw her understand. I saw her hesitate and then see there wasn't time for that. I yelled again, fiercely and with all my might, "Cut it!"

This time she reached inside and pulled out the cutters. It was hard to cut my end in the right place. I still had to hold on with my arms and legs or be dropped, dangling and useless in my rope harness. I fitted the cutters round the cable below

Rivet's rope harness and wedged the handles between my legs, so I could squeeze them closed and hold tight to the cable at the same time. I squeezed with every bit of strength I had. There was a deep clunk sound, and as the tension went out of the cable, I saw the cut end whipping back away from me, looking cruel, ready to cut a slash in the plane's skin. I swung for a moment, then Scanner must have cut her end and I was falling.

Everything went quiet, it seemed. It wasn't how I'd thought falling would be; slower, not frightening at all. I felt I was already part of another world. The sound of the plane and the gleam of its shiny body were already something I'd started to forget. Above me the sky was being sucked away, getting smaller, and the big green of the earth was rising all around. It was going to take me in and swallow me down, and I was glad of that now. Away to one side of me, against the green, I saw the silver wires and the explosive. The fall had pulled the wires from the plane and stripped the sheet of explosive from the cable. I watched them fall together and wondered why they'd been so important to me. It seemed a long time ago already. Then there was a flash and a crack, and they were gone.

nero

YEARS ago, when I was a little kid, a Rebel bomb took out the *Mandraya*'s sister ship. Fortay had been a pilot for just six months but he was smart enough to see that things were getting serious. He knew there'd come a time when he'd need to get in and out of the City quietly, without refueling anywhere obvious. The number of Stations had been falling for years, as Workers deserted, and the number of routes that craft needed to fly had contracted. There had been no reason for anyone to fly north of the City for at least five years. So that's where Fortay looked for his emergency fuel dump. He found a runway, owned by a minor family that had died out years before. It was tiny and derelict, not mentioned on any map or chart he had ever seen. Perfect! The first chance he got, he landed there with eight drums of aviation fuel and hid them in the bunker at the end of the concrete. The only time he ever went back was when he was teaching me to pilot the *Uccello* and we flew over it.

"Only you and I know about this, little bro," he told me. "Nobody from the City even looks this way, let alone flies here!"

In spite of what Fortay said, flying at altitude this close to the City made me feel too visible. So I brought the *Uccello* in low, to search for his dump. I remembered that it was hard to spot when you were flying low, being hidden between two long, hilly ridges; but all the same, I was nearly panicking by the time I found it. Our fuel was so low that we almost fell the last couple of feet onto the ground.

The runway was cracked and broken, which was why the strip had been forgotten, but it still felt too risky to be in the open. We got the *Uccello* in the hangar as fast as we could, taxiing her slowly between piles of rubble, with Bead and Spadey hauling the rusted doors closed behind us. I shut down the engines. Without the anxiety of the flight, the search for the dump and the landing, there was nothing left to keep my mind off Sacks.

I peeled out of the cockpit and climbed down into the hangar, where the Rebels were unloading whatever gear they'd snatched in the flight from the settlement. They all looked exhausted, and Sacks' death seemed to hang over everything like fog. I couldn't think of anything to say to them, or anything I wanted to hear. Like a machine, I walked round the *Uccello* and inspected the damage. The poor little bird had a rip in her hull, where the steel cable had recoiled, and enemy bullets had damaged the second starboard engine. It was two days' work, or maybe three, to repair it. Time to think what to do next. The hook and bait plan hadn't worked and now I had no way of telling who the string-puller had been; who had really been responsible for Fortay's death, not just Hasp who pulled the trigger. But at least I had the *Uccello* back. As for the Rebels? I'd have to find a way to let them go, get them out of the mess I felt I'd got them into.

I was so busy inside my head that I didn't see Rivet come and stand beside me. He was sucking on the corner of a foil Meal pack that must have been inside his overalls all the time. If Sacks had been that organized when she left the Station, maybe none of this would have happened. Maybe she and I would still be out there, walking on the prairie.

"Grubber's all right with a blowtorch," he said, looking at the holes in my bird. "We'll have it done in a couple of days."

"Right."

Rivet took a last pull on his Meal pack, then put it back inside his overalls with a sigh. We stood looking at the holes in the hull without seeing anything.

"I did give her a chute," said Rivet. "She wouldn't just have fallen."

"Give it up, Rivet. She's dead. You saw the explosion, same as I did. Chute or not, she was right on top of it."

"We could go and look for her?"

"What d'you think you'd find? She could be spread over a

hundred square miles."

"All right. All right. I get the message."

"What about Scanner?"

Rivet looked at his feet. "She's busy right now."

I didn't ask how she was busy. I knew: busy curled up somewhere, crying. "Fine," I said. "I'm going to take a look at the fuel dumps. Tell everyone else to keep under cover. We can't risk being seen." I turned to go but Rivet put a hand on my arm.

"Wait. Sacks said to give you this. She was worried she'd drop with it still on her." He shoved Sacks' little pouch into my hands.

"Oh that," I said, as if it didn't matter at all. "Thanks." I put it in a pocket and walked away.

Sacks' little pouch sat next to my heart like a weight. I couldn't bear to get it out and look at it. I wished Rivet had just kept it. I wanted a distraction and I didn't want to talk to anyone. The fuel dumps were under two broken-down huts on the other side of the runway. The open space of concrete between the hangar and the first hut was flooded in sunlight. A speck of dust blowing across it would be visible to a craft a thousand metres up. Crossing that space in broad daylight was very bad strategy. And way too scary. So I just ran across it without thinking, just feeling the fear and being grateful that, for a moment, I didn't have room to think about Sacks. *She could be spread over a hundred square miles.*

There was nothing left of the first hut; just three tin walls, a roof fragment and no fuel. I crossed the fifty feet of sunlit space to the next hut, before my heart rate had time to drop. It felt safer in hut two: there were four walls and a roof. I pulled up the trapdoor in the floor and dropped into the dusty little space beneath. Eight fuel drums, but only four of them full. Fortay must have called in sometime. But four was better than nothing. We could move them after dark. I climbed back out of the hole and dropped the trapdoor. Not a great start but something. At least the *Uccello* would be able to fly somewhere, if we could fix her.

I got ready to make the return sprint to the hangar. *Do it before you think any more, Nero.* I slid through the door and looked back the way I'd come. Whoa! It was like a hundred miles across that concrete, now! I drew back into the nice, safe shade and closed my eyes. Then I heard a buzzing, far above in the blue sky. I put my eye to a hole in the tin wall and there, in the western sky, was a dot; an unmistakable dot; an instantly familiar dot. It got closer, and changed into a pointy craft with swept-back black wings. It landed on the broken-down runway so fast, I couldn't even think about getting to the hangar and yelling, "Run! Just run!" It taxied and stopped. Its door opened.

I watched as five heavily armed Nabisco guards and three armour-clad Supas ran out and into the hangar. They were all holding weapons – the same batch of repeating automatic guns

I'd had in my workshop only last week, for routine maintenance and repairs. Why hadn't I welded the safety catches on, or slightly bent the barrels? My knees gave out and I leant on the hut wall, staring out through a crack and waiting for the shots. They didn't come. I listened hard, but there was nothing.

What happened instead was that two more figures came out of the little pointy craft. One was my father. No surprise there. When had either Fortay or I managed to do anything he hadn't somehow known about? The other guy was the shock. It was Hasp. He walked down the ramp beside my father. Side by side they looked really alike: both stringy, with the kind of straight stance you get from telling people what to do all the time. They were talking, and although Hasp didn't look too happy, he didn't seem to be my father's prisoner either. Still side by side, they disappeared into the hangar.

I sat down on the floor of the fuel hut. Why would Father be friendly with Hasp? There was one answer, but it seemed crazy: *my father, Scurro, had been the guy on the other end of the string.* Why would my father risk one of his few remaining craft, and his two sons, just to haul in a couple of dozen Rebels? It couldn't be true. Then I remembered what Fortay had told me about our father, on the morning of the Station 27 raid: *He refused to give me extra men!* Wouldn't that be exactly what Scurro would do, if we were being set up? A cold hole opened up inside me at that thought. I tried to unthink it, to push it away, but it wouldn't go. I had to find out what was going on.

I debated with myself for a while about how to get back to the hangar. Could I escape their notice if I crawled really slowly? Probably not. Was there a chance they wouldn't see me if I just went for it, fast, in one go? Maybe. Probably versus maybe. Great choice.

I chose maybe and ran round the back of the huts in an arc, to the rear of the hangar. I hit the black shade on the hangar's north side, with my heartbeat almost blowing my head apart. *Wow*, I thought, *I've made it*. I crouched low in the shadow and found a slit in the wall to look through, but all I could see was another bit of tin wall where the slit had been patched. I was just shuffling quietly to another slit when I heard the thick, distinctive click of my father's customized Colt 76 at the back of my head.

"Never cross open ground in daylight," he said. "Didn't the incompetent Fortay teach you anything? Now get up!" And he poked the barrel into my back, as kind of extra encouragement.

A hot lump of anger rose in my throat. "Great way to treat family, Father."

"That remains to be seen, Nero. Now, walk where I tell you."

He could make long-winded speeches over dinner, at family gatherings, but when it came to the sharp end of business, Scurro was a guy of few words. He walked me across the broken runway and into the hangar.

I couldn't make any guesses about how he'd found us. Some sort of tracking device on the plane perhaps. I'd always thought that kind of technology was part of the golden age of the past, but maybe Scurro had found something that still worked and somebody who knew how to operate it. Maybe they'd followed us all the way. I hadn't checked our airspace once after we lost the craft with Hasp on board. One thing was sure: Scurro wasn't pleased with me at all.

Father had brought serious support: Uncle Osso, solid as a truck and armed to the teeth, his sons Braccio and Notte, copies of their dad, plus another five of the regular hired muscle. They all stood in a circle around the Rebels, whose hands had been tied and whose mouths had been taped over. In spite of that, they were managing to look fierce and angry rather than plain terrified, like me. Nobody said anything, or even moved, so you could hear the scraping of the wind moving over the tin roof. I tried a smile at Scanner and Rivet but I don't think my face did what I told it to do. Hasp was sitting quietly to one side, on a fuel drum, looking comfortable and rather relaxed.

I coughed. I wasn't sure where to start my story or what story to tell, to save as many necks as possible, preferably including my own. I rehearsed a few in my head: *Dad, these Rebels have decided to fight on our side, so I was just bringing them to you... Father, I have recaptured the* Uccello *for the glory of the family.* I didn't get the chance to try any of them for real. Which was probably a good thing.

"Tie him," Uncle Osso ordered. Braccio stepped forward, grim-faced but a little uncertain. He was exactly between Fortay and me in age, and he'd always known us both.

"Braccio, please, just wait a second," I said.

Braccio hesitated, and we both looked at Scurro. Once again his quiet voice held everyone's attention. "Braccio, *tie him.*"

Braccio was a big guy and handled me as easily as if I had been made of cardboard. He drew my arms behind my back and tied my wrists together, but he did it gently, without hurting.

"Hasp has been helping us for some time, Nero," my father explained. "He offered to deliver to us a large number of Rebels, who were planning raids on more important Stations than 27."

I jerked free of Braccio and for a moment he let me go. I wanted to shout, but my throat had gone tight and narrow and just a little croak came out. "You used Fortay and me as bait?"

"No, the *Uccello* was the bait. The risk to Fortay was minimal. His death was ... unfortunate."

I looked at my father, at Osso and Notte. Their faces were blank. Only Braccio was fighting with his expression; he was thinking, like me: *Unfortunate? Is that all that Fortay was worth? Is that all those words about family come to?*

"What concerns me now," Scurro went on, "is that your actions at Hasp's camp disrupted our plans and betrayed

Nabisco interests, Nero."

"I was just doing what I needed to survive and get your craft back. You betrayed your sons!"

I didn't see the blow coming. I found myself on the floor at Osso's feet. "Braccio!" Osso barked. 'Search him!"

Braccio picked me up and did what he was told. He found Sacks' pouch on the first frisk and handed it to Scurro, who pulled out the blade and the firestarter without even glancing at them. He put his thin fingers inside the pouch and drew out a fragile sheet of paper, which I hadn't noticed the night I'd lit the prairie fire. It was old and greasy, and worn so thin that I could see the writing through it. There were just a few lines, but Scurro stared at them for several long minutes, his face getting tighter and paler all the time. Finally he crushed the paper in a single movement of his shaking fingers and dropped it to the floor like something poisoned. He stood quite still, staring ahead and breathing as if he had to think about it. The wind chafed at the rusted walls and we all waited for Scurro to speak, or explode or kill someone. The atmosphere was so tense, anything was possible.

At last he spoke, quite quietly but with a chill in his voice colder than anything I'd ever heard before. I shivered. "Your information was correct, Hasp," he said, and gave Osso the tiniest little nod. Immediately Osso took Hasp by the scruff of the neck. Hasp looked comically surprised, which I have to admit did give me a bit of a kick.

Scurro continued, the chill in his voice now expanded to an icy blast from a giant freezer. "Unfortunately your *incompetence* has lost us the girl. Without her, without *both* offspring, the chance of attracting the father is greatly reduced, even if you did have any real information about him."

Hasp began to talk fast, wriggling like a toy under Osso's massive grasp. "I've led you to him once before," he said. "Give me the boy and I will do it again."

"I have rather more concrete plans for my *ex-son*." Scurro turned away from Hasp, and Osso marched him outside.

Ex-son? I was bewildered and scared. My mind was racing, trying to make the words add up like columns of figures. *Lost us the girl ... without both offspring ... attracting the father...* But the only total I managed to reach was that there was a lot going on here that I didn't even begin to understand. I couldn't guess what Scurro would do next. I watched the colour return to his face and saw his mind begin to whirr again behind his blue eyes.

He turned to face me. "My only son, Fortay, is dead," he said. "You have never been my son."

I didn't like Scurro. Most of the time I was afraid of him, but those words still carried a punch that took my breath away. Scurro never said anything he didn't mean, and never went back on his word, so I knew my life – assuming I still had a life – had just changed totally, and for ever. It took me a second to realize he hadn't stopped talking.

"You and your new friends here, will do a job for me, or I will have you all killed." He didn't even pause for effect; it was matter-of-fact to him, just another piece of business. "There is a serious 'situation' between the families," he went on. "Very serious. I need to control the Murdoch propaganda system and all their other family resources, but principally the broadcast facility. If I challenge the head of their family openly, there will have to be war, which is in no one's interests. But there are certain Murdoch family members who would support a change of leadership, shall we say. They cannot be seen to be doing so, but if Fulton Murdoch were killed by a Rebel band ... and if my forces then came in and saved some small remnant of his people, no one would ask any questions. Timing is crucial. My mechanics will repair the *Uccello* while you prepare. You have three days." He turned away. "Find somewhere to lock them up," he told the guards.

The only place that was secure was the second shed. They taped my mouth like the others then put us all inside, with two guards posted outside. It was stuffy, with a sick smell of old fuel that made our noses run. We shuffled around for a while, trying to find comfortable places to sit or stand. I slumped down with my back to a wall and tried not to think. But it was impossible. Scurro's words and actions chased each other round in my head, along with all the opportunities I'd had – and hadn't taken – to read the paper from Sacks' pouch. If I had, surely I'd have a few more clues about what was going on?

After a while the guards' low chat outside told us they were settling down for a lazy afternoon in the sunshine. I shut my eyes. I didn't want to look at anyone. Someone nudged me in the ribs. I opened my eyes and saw Scanner's roasted little face grinning around her taped mouth. She made a little noise and tipped her head towards her feet. There, sticking out of the bottom of her trousers, was the crumpled paper from Sacks' pouch. I looked round the room. Everyone was focussed on that little knot of paper. Slowly, as quietly as possible, Bead slid towards Scanner's feet so his tied hands could reach the paper. I watched as his blind fingers felt for it, and started to unravel all the folds. Scanner pushed her feet out of her boots and helped with her toes, until the paper was spread out on the bottom of Bead's spine and held in place by Scanner's scarlet feet. I leant down, to bring my face close enough to read.

It was handwritten; a letter, or part of one. The writing was strong and sharp, so it was still readable, although the ink had faded to a kind of smudged purple:

Nabisco guards have found us. I've told Bly to go, to fight. To live. And the others, he's told to run, to hide, however they can. I'll stay here for the guards to find me. I think once they've got me and the boy, they'll leave the rest alone. I'm sure Scurro's ordered something more thorough, but his

*servants are getting lazy. They feel in their bones the deadness
of their own rule.*

*The truth is that this is the beginning of the end. The
Supas can't prevent it. Their words do not create reality as they
believe. The truth will defeat lies. Stations will lie in ruins, the
last City will fall. Hold on to this, don't despair!*

*Scurro's child dropped from my body, tiny and shapeless. I
buried it under the sky. So the girl child I'm sending you is
Bly's. Hide her, raise her like a Worker and keep her safe as
long as you can. Do whatever it takes. Her twin brother is with
me for Scurro to find. He won't kill a child that he believes is
his own, especially a son. This way they'll both be safe, hidden
in the system, my secret weapons, my children, who carry the
long truth of the prairie in their veins...*

I felt I'd been hit by something right in the exact centre of my
heart. *Her twin brother is with me for Scurro to find and take.
He won't kill a child he believes is his own, especially a son.
Her twin brother... Her twin brother...*

There was no date on the letter. Nothing to give away
where or when it was written. Except Nabiscos never used the
same name within two generations, or took a name another
family might use. The Scurro in this letter could only be one person. And this woman had been a lover ... or his wife. What did
I know about my mother? Scurro never even mentioned her.
Fortay told me things about her in whispers, when our father

wasn't around. There was something forbidden about her.

"She had dark skin, Nero, like you. I don't know where she came from. She wasn't a Supa and she wasn't a Worker."

"What happened to her, Fortay?"

"I don't know. She disappeared when she was pregnant. Father took four years to find her, but he only brought you back, not her. Don't ask me any more, Nero, please. That's all I can tell you."

All my life I'd searched my memory for something that might be a trace of my mother. All I found were rooms full of stern male relatives. Nights alone in the apartment. Days alone in my workshop, endlessly repairing things, endlessly improvising better ways for my family to kill people. Fortay sitting on my bed with some new geeky thing from the Low Tens.

My mother had always been dead in my mind, and I'd never had anyone to replace her. There were aunts and girl cousins, but at a distance, whispering, looking at me and looking away again. I knew their whispers were somehow about my mother, and I knew I wasn't allowed to ask about that. What did it matter, I told myself. Men were what counted in a Supa family. And yet I never seemed to count at all. But maybe there was something of those four first years I'd had with her stored inside me. Every time I'd watched the buffalo and the old guy flickering on my bedroom wall, I *had* remembered something. Not a face, or a voice, but a feeling; so strong, it seemed to run through me like blood. I'd got it that day on the prairie with Sacks too. A feeling I'd never put a name to. Until now. The feeling was *belonging, being myself.* Being where and who I *really* was. *My children, who carry the long truth of the prairie in their veins.*

The heat of the shed made my scalp sweat, and the fumes of fuel caught in my throat, but I didn't notice. I read those words over and over again, until I knew *my mother* had written them. Everything made sense. I didn't fit the Supas' world properly because I wasn't meant to. Scurro and I had never much liked each other because I was never his son!

It also made sense of the Station 27 raid. Scurro had risked so much because Hasp had offered him the chance of revenge. Somehow – I couldn't begin to know how – Hasp knew something about me and Sacks. Whoever this Bly guy was, Hasp knew Scurro would be keen to get hold of him. No wonder Hasp had been so pleased when Sacks and I just fell into his hands. He'd thought he'd blown it and we'd gone up in smoke with the Station!

I thought about Sacks then. I knew she couldn't have read the letter; brought up as a Worker, she couldn't read. She'd never known what it said, and yet, thinking of her, I could see that she had known who she was. She'd found the prairie running in her blood without needing to be told. It made me feel a little better about her somehow. At least Scurro couldn't use *her* as bait to settle old scores with his wife's lover.

I worked the tape on my mouth with my tongue and teeth

until I bit a hole in it big enough to speak through. Scanner silently leaned her ear to my mouth, so I could breathe the letter's words without the guards hearing. She sat staring at me for quite a while before she bit her way through her own tape to pass on what she'd heard. I watched carefully and saw that all Scanner seemed to pass on was three words: *He's Bly's son*. I caught them each time, and the gasp that followed. It was all I needed to let me know that Bly was a fighter, a Rebel leader, a kind of legend even.

At last they all sat, staring at me, astonished, impressed-looking. I stared back, feeling uncomfortable, and thinking that Nero Nabisco had got them into this mess and whoever Bly was, his son had to to get them out.

sacks

IN my sleep I was warm and dry, so I shut my eyes tight to keep the waking out. But a voice got into my ears all the same. "No good just lyin' in the mud," it said. "Have a little snifter to get you up." And then the neck of a cold bottle clattered on my teeth, and a burst of liquid flame came into my mouth. I sat straight up, coughing out mud and fiery drink by turns. I opened my eyes, but there was silty mess and blood over my face, and I still couldn't see.

"'Ere," said the voice. "Let's wash that off, eh?"

Hard fingers, like Mott's, grabbed me up and pushed my head into cold water, then pulled me up again. I struggled and tried to yell out.

"No call for all that noise. Still, 'tis a good job. I was thinking you was never going to speak!"

I spluttered the last of the water away and saw where I was: on a spit of mud beside a long smudge of brown water. Squatting in front of me, and looking into my face, was a woman far too large for her squeaky little voice. She was dressed in weird scraps of a kind of material I'd never seen before. There were brown bits, grey bits, rust-coloured and black bits, and, strung round her broad shoulders, fat rolls of fluffy black-and-white stripes. Dazed as I was, I couldn't take my eyes off them.

"These is all my catches. My furs," she said. "This 'ere's a fox. Caught him in the frost, up by the river bend. That's a marmot, these is deers' skins, and all these is my raccoon tails!" She shook her huge shoulders so the striped pieces jiggled and her black hair swished. She laughed, and took a swig from the bottle of fiery drink. "I like the tails best. They're my favourite. D'you like 'em then?"

I nodded.

"Don't look like you do," she said, and stuck out her bottom lip in a little pink shelf.

"I do," I said, though my voice didn't seem to be up to much. "Just, I don't feel so good." I had to lie down again then, on the wet and cold mud. I couldn't seem to keep sitting, because of the aches in me and the throbbing in my head. I closed my eyes.

But the woman wasn't ready to stop talking. She leant down close to my face and pulled an eyelid open.

"Look there," she said, pointing up a green slope rising steep above us.

A great billow of material and a tangle of strings was caught among the plants at the bottom. *Rivet's chute!* I thought.

"'Tis no wonder you feel so bad," she continued. "Fell down there with your chute dragging for half a mile."

I could make out a sort of line in the greenery, but I couldn't keep my eyes open.

"You're lying in that mud again!" she scolded. "I *said* not to!" Then she picked me up in her great brown arms and carried me to a thing like a long, narrow crate. "I found you, so you'll come with me in my canoe on the river."

She laid me in the bottom of it, and pushed it out onto the water. Even with her great weight inside, the "canoe" floated, like the Alien's feather had floated on the pond. My head rested at one end and my legs stretched to where the woman knelt, pushing a flat pole into the "river" on one side and then the other. I could feel how the woman's pushing with the pole made us go forward. The water pattered on the sides of the canoe by my ears, and the woman's voice trailed around us as we went along. High notes and low, with words too. I'd never heard such singing. She sang the same thing over and over, so I came to hear what the words were:

"Oh, Shenandoah, I long to see you.
Away, you rolling river.
Oh, Shenodoah, I long to see you.
Away, I'm bound to go,
Cross the wide Missouri."

I wondered if her singing showed in the air somehow, like a line of feathers caught in the wind.

"Look at 'er Missouri, just look!" It was getting dark, as well as cold and wet now. The water was still slapping the canoe on one side, but we'd stopped moving. "Just look!" The voice was a man's and all riled up, by the sound of it. A light shone right at my face and I tried to turn away, but my head was too heavy. "You shouldn't have just laid her in the bottom of the canoe, Missouri! She isn't one of your baby otters or some old eel!"

"I didn't have time for anything else, Kai. I brought her 'ere, didn't I?"

I could hear that the woman had stuck out her bottom lip again.

The man's voice softened, "Yes, you did. We'll care for her now, Missouri."

"You do more'n care for her," said the woman, as I felt myself gently lifted from the boat. "You take a good *look* at 'er. We've seen her before, you and me and Bly." And the woman gave a strange low giggle.

"What *are* you on about, Missouri?" The man was half laughing himself, half cross.

"You just wait. I'll be back to see her, when I've done gathering some news for you!"

I heard her get into the canoe and paddle away, then the

strands of her song started to drift on the cold breeze.

"Can you hear me?" asked the man, soft-voiced now.

"Yes," I whispered.

"Good. That's very good. Right, I'm going to take you up to the village. I'll have to carry you... I'll try not to hurt."

All of me was covered in cuts and scratches, and everything inside felt slapped and rattled. So, as he struggled along the path with me, every move was a new pain. But he was being kind so I tried not to to make a sound.

It was hard to see the village at all. The huts had all but disappeared into the dusk, but I could make out where each one was, when the lights inside shone out. It wasn't like the Rebels' settlement. There was nothing from the Supas' world here: no bits of Station that I could see, just rows of arched huts blending in with the air around them, and behind that, I thought I could see *trees*! Not quite like the ones on Home, which TV showed, but trees they were, for sure. Was Home real after all then? And had I come to it?

"Missouri found 'er," my man was telling a girl my age. She had dark hair and dark eyes that she rolled at him, like I used to do at Mott.

"Oh Da-ad! She could be *anything* ... a spy or whatever."

This got the man angry again, and he snapped at her. "She's half dead, is what she is, so don't give me cheek. Run and tell Bly I need some help."

The girl didn't stop to say more, but ran off as the man

Missouri called Kai carried me inside a hut.

Inside there was one room with a round roof. Little flames on sticks hung in holders and lit the place up. There was a table, a couple of stools and a big bed. The bed was covered in furs and Kai laid me on them. They were soft, and didn't smell like Missouri's did, of damp and dying. Kai gathered up the flame sticks, and brought them round the bed, to give more light, and then sat looking at me. He had a round, flat face, with a little snub of a nose and a wide mouth.

"You look like Mott," I told him, but my voice was too weak for him to hear, so he just smiled at me and said, "Shut your eyes and rest. I'll dress your cuts and scratches when you've settled."

He had a smile like Mott too, so I felt sad all over again that Mott was gone and that I was lost, with no Station, no friends, alone in the great Outside. I began to cry. "You're like Mott," I said again, as loud as I could, and this time he heard me.

"Like *Mott*?"

I nodded.

"You wait there," he said. "I'll be back!" And he jumped up and ran out of the door.

There were voices talking over me again. I didn't like it. It made me feel like I was already dead. But now my eyelids were far too heavy to think of lifting them, so I lay and listened to two men talking. The first I hadn't heard before. It was a quiet voice, but sharp-edged and clear. It made me think of Nero.

"Where did Missouri find her?" the clear, soft voice said.

"In the mud at the bottom of Green Cut." This was a deeper voice and rougher. It was Kai, the man who'd brought me to the village. "Missouri said she'd broken a path of saplings all the way down from top to bottom with a 'chute'."

"Well, it's a while since we saw one of those! You sure she said 'Mott'?"

"Sure as I stand here, Bly. It's what she said."

"Did you look to see if she's anything on 'er. An object, a letter – anything."

"Nothing. Just Station issue clothes, but *man's* clothes. So Mott was still doing what he was asked."

"It could be another Mott."

"Another Mott? What? And another girl the right age? Look at her Bly! She's the image of her mother! What's happened to you? Don't you believe anything any more?"

"I believe –" Bly gave a long, long sigh – "I believe that … that this kid needs our help now, no matter who she is. All right, Kai?"

"Winema Bly. Have it your way."

"Good."

"Well, let's take a look at her." Kai was all bustle now. "Phoenix! Phoenix! Get the salves and bandages from my pack!"

But before any footsteps came running, Bly called out,

"No need for that, Phoenix. I've brought some with me." And then he said, quietly so I thought maybe only I heard, "I'll dress her wounds for her." I didn't hear any more for a while then.

When at last I managed to open my eyes a little, there was a skinny, tall man leaning over me. His hair was dark, tied back the way I'd seen some Rebels wear it, and his face was all angles: his nose, cheeks, forehead and mouth were like something made from scrap metal. His skin looked like he might have a layer of Scanner's burnt redness underneath the brown of it, but it was a good bit lighter than mine. His hands were gentle and steady, and he cleaned every cut and scratch, and bound them up so they didn't hurt so much. He gave me a drink that he said would help the pain. When he was done, he and Phoenix put me in soft clothes that didn't press my skin. Then Phoenix went out and left the tall man, Bly, by my bed.

"How do you feel now?" He spoke softly, and leaned close to hear me answer.

"Better."

"Could you talk a little?"

I nodded.

"OK. Good. I don't know your name!"

"Sacks."

"Sacks. Sacks." He said it a few times. Turned it over in his mouth, looking for some taste or other. "Right," he said at last. "How did you get here, Sacks – I mean before Missouri found you?"

I didn't have the voice to say much, and my remembering of what had happened was muddled with hurt and tiredness. So I told him I'd fallen out of a plane, and before that I'd been on a Station that had burned down. He never asked what I was doing on a plane, or why the Station burned down. No. What he wanted to hear was *who* was on the Station with me. I told him once and then he asked again, like he didn't hear the first time.

"Mott?" he said. "The man on the Station with you was called *Mott*?"

"Yes."

"How long did you live on that Station? Half a year?"

"All my time. Mott said it was special, not to have to move."

He let out another big sigh, and got up and paced about the room. When he sat down again, he laid a hand on mine, and I could feel his steadiness was gone. But there was a comfort in his trembling fingers, and I fell asleep.

Phoenix was laughing at me. I was sucking the last taste of food off my fingers. "What *was* that?"

"Cornbread, made out of what we grow in the fields – I'll show you tomorrow. And duck."

"Duck?"

"Yes, duck! One I caught down on the river yesterday. Duck, you know?" she said, pushing her arms out to her sides and moving them up and down. "You *know*, quack quack!"

I laughed at her, though I still didn't understand what she was telling me. Bly came and sat beside us on the grass outside Kai's hut, "I'm sorry to stop the fun, Phoenix, but your dad wants you up at the corn garden."

"Now?"

"Yes, I think so."

"Can Sacks come?"

"Later maybe."

"Oh. OK, Winema Bly. See you later, Sacks. Quack quack!"

We watched her run off between the huts, still waving her arms and making that silly sound! It took me a little while to stop laughing. "Bly, what's a 'duck'?" I asked.

"I suppose you'd be told it was a sort of Alien, an Earth native."

"A living being then?"

"Yes, a kind of being we call a bird."

"I seen birds. With Mott. They have feathers!"

"That's it. A duck is a kind of bird."

"And that's what I've eaten?"

Bly nodded and I sat quietly, thinking of how I'd felt watching the white crane rising into the sky and of Mott rubbing his belly and laughing at me.

"You don't like the thought of eating a bird?"

I shook my head. "It makes me sad. But it's better than

eating Product that Units make. They're not even properly alive before they die. Units are birds, aren't they?"

Bly nodded sadly. "Yes, 'fraid so. Birds that Supas have done terrible things to."

"I found a feather on one. That's how I knew. That's how I first thought..."

"Thought what, Sacks?"

"There's no Home, is there, Bly?"

"Not like Supas say. No, there isn't."

"Thought not." We sat in silence. I wasn't sure if I felt better or worse knowing *for absolutely sure* that Home was just a clever story. "Humans didn't come from somewhere else, did they?" I said. "They've always been here, isn't that right?"

Bly nodded. "Could you walk a little way?" he asked. "I want to show you something."

It was a warm day, the part of the year that Bly called Summer. We walked out of the village, away from the grass-roofed huts and into the trees. I loved the trees; the sound the air made going through them, and the way they cut the light into pieces and threw it on the ground below. I wanted to stop and look, but Bly said there'd be time for that another day.

We came out from the trees and into a grassy place, where the ground got steeper. Huge grey slabs poked out from the green. Bly said these were rocks, the bones of the Earth, like the bones in our own bodies but older, more lasting. Rocks had been this way for almost all of time. Bly led me through a gap between two rocks, like the door of a building. Inside, a rock slab, big as a Station wall and smooth on one side, stretched up. "Look at the rock, Sacks."

It was shady and the light was low so I stared at the grey rock, seeing only a fuzz of nothing. Then my eyes took to the gloom and I saw pictures! Hundreds of them, looking as if they had been there for the whole long life of the rocks. It wasn't like TV; you couldn't see the pictures move, and there weren't colours or anything. They were just little black outlines of things, but as clear and alive as the day and the trees. They showed living beings of all sorts – birds, animals – all together with people.

"Who made these pictures, Bly?"

"My people, Outsiders. People who lived in this place a long, long time ago. Just the way we live here now."

I looked hard at the pictures. Sometimes the people ate the animals, and sometimes the animals ate each other, but they all seemed to go on running around together. "What happened? Why didn't it stay like this?"

Bly walked the length of the rock, holding his hand against the greyness so he brushed it with his palm. "I don't know it all, Sacks. Don't think any living being knows it all now. But a long time ago, people – humans – covered the Earth almost all over with Cities, and most of what wasn't covered in cities was poisoned by what flowed out of them. The ground wouldn't grow plants, the air wasn't fit to breathe and the rain was toxic. Thousands, maybe millions, of people died – animals too. Those that were left were very afraid.

"That's how the Supas took things over. They were the richest, the most powerful families. They had the resources to build crystal domes to protect their Cities and grow food inside vast buildings, Stations. But they needed Workers to grow their food and to run their Cities – building, mending, cleaning... All the things Supas didn't want to do. So they offered ordinary people a choice: stay Outside and take your chances with the poisoned world or become a Worker. And folk were so scared to be left Outside that they fought to get into the Stations and the Work Houses in the Cities.

"Once they were inside, families were split apart. Children were taken from their parents to work as soon as they could walk. Supas knew families made people strong and they wanted people they could push about. And that's what they got – people so scared and broken, they were grateful to be slaves. But the Workers didn't stay grateful, once they saw who was getting the best of the deal. So Supas started using violence and drugs – Product – to keep the Workers where they wanted 'em. And you know about Product don't you!"

I nodded, and shivered to remember how I'd felt without it. "I was lucky I didn't die without it!" I said.

Something passed over Bly's face then, a kind of shadow, and he touched my cheek with the ends of his long fingertips. Then he went on, "It all worked smoothly enough for a while, with Workers kept down and quiet. But then Supas began to fight and quarrel among themselves. Whole Cities just disappeared in bombs and fighting. The Cities that survived began to fail. Supas had the power, but they didn't have the knowledge. When buildings crumbled, they didn't know how to rebuild 'em. When machines failed, they didn't know how to mend them. And if Workers knew how, they mostly weren't telling any more!

"All this time something else was going on. With the Cities failing, there wasn't so much poison getting in the air and water. Slowly, over the years and years, the Earth began to heal. The land that had been dead and wasted came alive, the prairie grew back and the woods started to sprout! Workers that broke away to Outside now lived, and started to make real trouble for the Supas. Supas got more and more scared. And the scareder they got, the more Product they put in Meals. That kept Workers addicted to Product, tied to Meals and the Stations, where they knew they could get them. But it didn't make them afraid to go Outside. Supas needed Workers to be terrified of Outside, to believe it was toxic. So they invented Planet Home and the idea that we humans never belonged on this planet. They fed it to the Workers on their TVs, and it worked as good as Product to keep Workers in slavery!"

"Was everyone who wasn't a Supa a slave then? A Worker?"

"No, most, but not everyone. Some always stayed Outside.

Supas and their Cities didn't kill everything. There were always places where the water was clean enough, where the soil would grow something; that's where my people, the Outsiders, hung on, living by the ways of these pictures." He patted the rock and its endless dance of people and animals. "They waited for times to get better. For the Supas' days to pass. And now they are nearly passed."

"I wish I was part of your people that had always lived Outside. I wish I'd never had to live on a Station and dream of lies."

Bly looked into my face as if there were pictures to see, like on the rocks. "But you *are* a part of this. Let's go and sit out where its warm. I need to tell you some more."

I sat beside him, and the warmth that the sun gave the rock, the rock gave back to me as I listened to Bly's story; my story.

"I was born out on the prairies," he began," out in the big grass under the wide skies, far away from any Stations or Cities. That's where my people had always lived; huge families of us – Sioux, Mandans, Dakotas, the Old Folk. They'd stayed Outside, right through the bad times when Earth was sick and the animals and people were dying. That's when most people went into Cities or inside Stations. But those old families, they stayed out along with a few Workers who had the courage for it. Many of them died. Whole families were lost and their names forgotten. But not all. By my grandfather's time, things were healing up, and life for us Outside was easier. The families had mixed by then but we called ourselves by the same name, Outsiders. There were other Outsiders too, in the mountains in the west, in deserts to the far south, and up north on the ice. The ice folk were called the Inuit – that's where Kai's people came from and your Mott's too.

"I grew up knowing how to live from the prairie *and* how to keep out of the way of Supas, and all their badness. About the time when I was born, things were getting worse and worse for the Cities. There was only one left that we knew about on this part of the planet. Workers were escaping but most of them got lost or starved, or died through having no Product. But not all, and those that lived started making trouble: burning Stations, raiding delivery craft, even attacking the Cities. Supas started venturing out of their buildings and their vehicles, searching for Rebels to catch and kill. But they never came out as far as us, until one day three aero-craft came over our village. They had bombs and guns, and they didn't care that we weren't Rebels. What they hated was that we were living free. They hated us because we were Outsiders, more dangerous to them, in a way, than Rebels.

"They killed almost everyone. All my family died. My parents and my two sisters, my grandfather, and my mother's brother and his family. A few children survived, and they picked us out of the ashes and took us to work in the City. I never knew what happened to the other children. Knowing who they were, I'd guess they made a lot of trouble and got themselves killed. But I didn't make trouble at all. I put all my anger and my crying inside, where the Supas couldn't see it, and I planned and wished. If wishes could break walls, their City would have been dust and blood the moment I got there."

Bly's voice had flowed evenly and softly like the air moving in the trees. But now it flared up and lit his thin face. I saw that under his steadiness there was something fierce, like a blade made of the hottest fire. But as soon as it at flickered it was gone, and he went on with the story.

"I kept quiet and I learned everything I could about the Supas' world. Everything. By knowing it, I'd know how to smash it. Or so I thought then. I was a good Worker, a Worker who they thought wanted nothing more than to be like a Supa. I learned how to mend their cars. They've forgotten how to make new ones, like they've forgotten so much else. So they need to keep the old ones going. They prize a good mender, a mechanic. They prized me so highly, they looked aside when I didn't take Meals any more and broke my addiction to Product. They prized me so highly, that Nabisco himself bought me to take care of all his family cars. And that's how I met your mother. She was called Onida."

I knew how humans were made. I knew I'd come out of a woman's belly before I came to be with Mott. But mothers, fathers, brothers and sisters were what Supas had. Those words were part of Supas' power, part of what made them strong and made us 'just Workers', less than machines. "My mother," I said, trying the word to see how it might fit in my mouth. But I could only say it once, as I found my voice was gone.

Bly went on. It seemed almost like a fever in him now, this story that he had to get to the end of. "She was Nabisco's new wife. His third. She was brought up on a Station far to the south. A Station that was free – had been right from the start. Onida called it 'the Pueblo'. The people there, her people, she said had been slaves, long long ago, back before the Poisoning. They were the ones who gave her her dark skin, darker than yours even! But when the Poisoning came, they joined families of old Outsiders, the Hopi and the Navaho, and started their free Station, their Pueblo. It was like one of our Outsider settlements really, but it made fuel for cars and aeroplanes. The Pueblo people traded with the Supas. Supas didn't like them much, but Scurro Nabisco wanted to make sure he'd always have fuel, even if no one else did. And the Pueblo people wanted to keep on the right side of the Supas, so your mother didn't have a choice. She was traded along with the fuel.

"The Pueblos didn't know much about how Supas ran their world, so Onida learned some hard things in her first year in the City. I was her driver. I took her all over. Sometimes with him, but more and more on her own. We talked. She'd been sold like a barrel of oil but she wouldn't flow like the oil did! Scurro tried to make her change her name, but she wouldn't and he beat her for it. "Onida," she told me. "I won't stop being Onida, 'the searched-for one'." She was frightened – she guessed Scurro had had his first two wives killed.

"I was part of a secret Rebel group by then: Workers and a few of the Old Folk – Outsiders. Sioux, Algonquin, Inuit, some other families too. Kai was one. We planned to blow up the TV tower because we knew it was as bad for workers as Product was. But we were betrayed. Kai and I had two hours to escape the City. I went to Onida and asked her to come with us. She did. She left everything behind, all her comfort and wealth, everything she knew. Everything.

"We got out of the City, Kai, Onida and me, and kept moving. It was hard. Travelling on foot and by night, in the cold and rain of autumn. Onida lost Scurro's child she was carrying. But she was glad to be rid of it, she said, because it was his and not mine. She was fierce in her feelings, Onida. Scared me at times. We kept going, but I feared winter would kill her if we didn't find some sort of settlement. There was a Rebel village built of scraps of Stations, surviving on the leavings of Supas. Many of them were still addicted, still on Product, so they needed to raid Supa outposts. Every time they did, they risked their lives – and the Supas' revenge. Kai and I showed them how to get free from Product, how to live from the Earth without Supas. We told them 'now you're free to bring the Supas' world down!'

"As soon as it was spring we moved the village, took it far away from the Supas' routes and Stations. You and your brother were born in the new place, late one summer night, with a warm wind and a sky full of stars. It seemed like a blessing, a sign that everything would work out well. We called you Wichapi and your brother Tadewi, the Old Folk's words for star and wind, the freest beings in the universe." Bly's steady voice shook and clogged to a stop. He breathed slowly and deeply and looked at me.

"So you are..." I couldn't say the words.

Bly croaked them for me. "I am your father. Onida was your mother."

It was too hard to look in his eyes, so I was glad that he turned away and wiped his face with his hands. "Shall I go on?" he asked, and I nodded.

"Nabisco couldn't leave what he believed he owned. He never gave up searching for Onida and his child that had been inside her. It took him four years to find her, or maybe four years to get someone to betray us. I don't know which. Anyway, a lookout spotted the craft far off, so we had a little time to decide what to do. We had bunkers hidden under the grass, where we could hide from passing craft, but determined searchers on the ground would find us in there, and kill us like rats in a bag. So we chose to hide the young and the old in the bunkers, but the rest of us would have to run and fight, to draw the searchers away and make them believe they'd found all there was to find. Whatever we did, we knew it was the end of our life there and that many of us were going to die that day.

"Your mother knew it was her and the child the men were

really after. If she hid with you two, the men would kill every-one to find her. So she said she'd stay in the village, with your brother. Once Nabisco's men found them, she was sure they'd leave us alone. 'He'll be pleased with a boy,' she said. I left Onida with Tadewi and I put you, Wichapi, in a bunker with a Worker spy, who said there was a Station he could take you to. That Worker was called Mott and he could be trusted to keep you hidden, inside the system. You'd be brought up as a Worker child, and be safe that way. I couldn't bear the thought of it, but your mother was determined. She was a fierce woman. 'This is the only way,' she said. 'We're all going to live, I know it.' She believed it so strongly.

"So I walked from the village, from my Onida and my Tadewi, and dropped the lid of the bunker on you, my sweet, sweet daughter.

"Then I went with some of the men and women of the village to fight, and draw Nabisco's men away. Onida shouted after me, 'You are not to die. We will live and be with our children again!'

"I've thought of that every day and tried to believe it. But until now I couldn't."

Bly wiped the tears off his face again. He did a poor job, leaving the hollows of his cheeks still wet. He was a tall, straight man, but he leant elbows on knees and head on hands as if he'd fall to bits if every part wasn't resting on another. I sat stiff and cold in the warm sunshine. The story he'd told, which was also *my* story, lay inside me like a dead thing. Bly had told me so much, but I felt it was nothing like enough. At last I thought of questions to ask, but every answer just made us both more sad.

"What happened to Onida and Tadewi?"

"I don't know. I never had Onida's faith in survival. I believe Nabisco guessed the boy wasn't his and killed him. I've heard reports of a youngest son, but..." Bly looked at his hands and shook his head sadly. "I think my boy is dead. And Onida too. Nabisco killed his first two wives, and Onida was always afraid of him."

Lost I thought, *all lost*. And through the cold in me a scald of anger rose up, like oil on water. What was the good of this story to me now? Everything in it had been lost from the moment the four of us had been separated. From that moment, I was no longer Wichapi, child of Bly and Onida, but someone else. What was the point of telling Bly about Nero's dark, narrow face, his deep brown eyes? Tadewi *was* as good as dead: he'd become another person. It was all too late.

Bly tried to take my hand and I snatched it away. I stood up and faced him and cried out, "Why didn't you keep us with you?"

Bly took the words like a blow to the heart. "We had seconds to decide," he whispered. "To decide what was the best way to keep you both from dying! We thought it was the only chance to keep you *alive*!"

"But if we'd died, we'd have been with you and her. We'd

have died as *ourselves*. Not lived like we have. Never belonging, being someone else. You *made* your son be Scurro Nabisco's son, and I'm ... *this*. All I know is the inside of a Station. And I'm *old*, so old, when I should be like Phoenix, running like she runs, laughing like she laughs! '

"I'm sorry. Oh, Wichapi."

"Don't call me that. Wichapi's *dead*. I'm Sacks!"

I left Bly standing at the rocks and ran down through the trees. Belonging to Planet Home had been so easy. This was what real belonging felt like: hard and hurting, giving no clues about what to do or where to go.

They left me alone in the hut all day. Once I heard Phoenix run down the path calling "Sacks" but someone hushed her and she went away again. Bly didn't try to speak to me, although I reckoned he might have been close by. Everything slapped around inside me, like the overalls in Mott's washing machine – first one colour coming to the top then another. But after a while it was Nero that came to the top of the tumble most often. And the more he did so, the more I thought how we were alike, lost as we were between two names. If I belonged anywhere, it was with Nero, if only to tell him who we both might have been. But how was I ever going to find him again?

I came out of the hut in the dark, feeling hungry now I'd settled on what to think. There was a bit of cornbread on the table outside, and I picked it up and looked around. There wasn't a sound or a sign of anyone. I suddenly felt afraid. Had I been asleep and missed the sounds of Supas coming to wreck Bly's world again? I walked up the path, past unlit huts, full of emptiness. I followed the spiral path, curling in tighter with each curve, and as the quiet went on and on I started to think I'd find something horrible around the next bend.

Up ahead I heard voices, raised and excited, but no shots or screams. Then I was at the end of the path, and in front of me was a big grassy space and everyone from the village standing in a circle around a centre, lit with lanterns and fire sticks. The people were packed in too tightly to push through and see what was happening. I thought I'd wriggle between them, but Phoenix came up behind me and took my hand. "Come 'ere," she whispered. "Chinook's got a ladder on her ma's roof. We can see it all from up there."

There were five or six kids already on the curved grass roof when Phoenix and I got up there. It was strange to be with so many people of my own age, but I was saved from feeling awkward as they didn't even look at me. They were all staring down at the lighted circle and the talking adults, like Workers sitting watching TV with their Meal.

A tall, thin woman, with hair cut close to her skull, was shaking her arms out in front of her as she spoke, as if she was holding her meaning up to be seen. "We can't keep out of it any longer!" she said, and the crowd murmured "no" and "yes" in equal part. "We want the City to fall, don't we?" The yeses drowned out the noes at the sound of this. I didn't understand any of it, not yet.

"We want the Supas' evils to be over for ever?"

Another lot of yeses, louder this time and quicker.

"Then we should help the Rebels."

Noes and yeses rippled backwards and forward like the weedy tangles in a tank.

A man with white hair and a grey beard came into the circle.

"Why should we help the Rebels? All they want is to be Supas themselves!"

At this loud yeses poked up from the crowd, like fists. I began to understand what they were talking about. The old man was right, that *was* what Rebels wanted, but only because they didn't know anything else. A woman stepped into the light and spoke up. She held a bundled-up baby in one arm. I had never seen a baby before and stared at its tiny face so hard, it seemed that the baby was speaking, not the woman. "How can we fight Supas? We don't have guns and aero-craft..."

Someone shouted out straightaway, sounding very excited. "But we have our courage!"

The crowd groaned, and I did too inside. I thought of that baby in the middle of a battle and remembered what Bly had said about the raid on his village *They killed almost everyone. All my family died.* When the old bloke spoke again, I felt he'd said my own thoughts.

"And what will courage be, when they come to bomb this village, eh? Keep out of it, I say. If the Supas fall now or in a hundred years, what does it matter to us?"

All words got drowned out then, in the fuss, as the crowd seemed to be arguing with itself, with much shouting and arm waving. Through the muddle of it I could see a jiggling ring of stripy tails, making a path through the people. It was Missouri pushing her way to the lit circle. She stood, waiting, shifting herself from one big foot to the other, until the crowd quieted down again. Then her loud, squeaky voice cut into the quiet.

"There's something big going on," she said. "I been right down the Hudson, I been across to the Sound. The lights is going out on all the skyscrapers in Manhattan. There's darkness all over at night, and burning." The crowd, silent now, gasped. "There's flames on the ground and up the tallest buildings. Bombs going off. Craft being shot down. Supas fighting Supas and Rebels everywhere. There's Rebels all along the bottom of the Sound, camped in the bays, hiding out. Hundreds of 'em, thousands maybe, getting ready." Missouri's face shone and her teeth showed in a grin. "The City's going down," she declared, "for sure!"

Voices jumped up loudly after that. Missouri stayed in the circle, looking pleased that she'd made everybody so noisy. But there was a scared, panicky feel to the noise, and I felt my hairs stand on end. Then Kai and Bly stepped into the light together. They didn't have to wait for quiet. It came straight away, and I could see every face catching the light and turned towards them.

Kai spoke first. "You aren't going to like what I've got to tell you," he said, and everyone sort of drooped, although they didn't make a sound. "You all know we've had scouts out west of the City this last month. Their news isn't good. It's swarming with armed Supas, way off their normal routes. They've poisoned all the lakes, so there's dead animals all over. Dead people too. We found thirty Rebels, new escapees still in their Workers' issue, at Bear Lake. The Supas are scared. They're fighting themselves and they're fighting the Rebels. The more scared they get, the further they'll go from their flight paths and their roads. They'll poison all the water sources they can't control. We won't be safe here much longer."

No one said a word. Kai looked down at his feet. It seemed it was Bly's turn now. He stepped forward and there were little whispers of that word I'd heard Phoenix and Kai call him – 'Winema'.

"Phoenix," I breathed, "why do they call him that, Winema?"

"Its an Old Folk's word. It means chief, boss man."

The moment Bly began to talk, the crowd was different. It seemed like he truly was Winema. Bly used his words like he used his hands for mending my hurts – steady and safe. His words and his fingers might quake in dealing with his own life,

173

but in leading others' lives, he was sure and solid. I saw now that was why he'd left me behind with Mott.

"You all know what I've always said," he began. "We're close to Manhattan and that's been our strength: Supas won't look so close to home. They've probably never noticed this little gap on their maps. But they're going to notice it now. Old Tahetan is right, Supas *are* going down, their time *is* done, but they'll take us with them if we let them go down slowly. Who knows how much of the land they'll poison out of fear and spite? Manhattan is the last of the Cities along the eastern coast. We've got to finish it, and finish it fast to keep this part of the land safe. We, the Outsiders, we're the ones who have to lead the way so that Rebels and Workers don't just start to be a new sort of Supa."

Bly stopped and let the little ripple of folk agreeing with him die down. When he spoke again his voice was quieter, and it seemed that people held their breath to hear.

"I think some of you know that Kai and I have more work to do in the world than what we do here. This is the time we've been planning for many long years." *So*, I thought, *you did go on fighting, even though you seemed so peaceful here.* 'We'll be leaving shortly," he said, louder now. "Them that want to can come with us. We'll scout the lakes and head for Manhattan City. There's a lot blades and stealth can do that guns and bombs can't stop. Everyone else, pack for travel up to the Rondaks. You've done longer journeys before. Winter before last, most of us followed the deer for two months. Three summers ago, we spent almost back on the prairie, to raise a good crop of corn and take the buffalo." He left a little pause so the crowd could remember what must have been good times, then added, calm, warm, strong. "This is no different."

For a while no one said a thing, then Tahetan, the man with white hair, yelled out, "What does he mean he's been planning? I thought we didn't have chieftains 'ere? Why's he telling us what to do?"

No one bothered to shout Tahetan down. Just one young man took his arm and told him straight, "Nobody's giving orders, old man, but we do have one chieftain, Winema Bly, and he's just talking the sense that we all know is true, and doing the job he's always been doing while he's been with us. Now get packing."

People picked up their lanterns and fire sticks, and the round of light broke up into little pools that followed the paths to the huts. The children slid off the roof, and I followed Phoenix down. She ran to Kai. He was standing with Bly and Nomis, Phoenix's mother. The light of Kai's lantern held them all together, and I hung back out of the glow.

"Mum!" said Phoenix, and wrapped her arms around Nomis' waist.

"It's all right, Phoenix." Nomis comforted her. "We'll be back to pick the corn you've been growing. Don't you worry."

Kai grinned and ruffled Phoenix's hair. "Bly and I are used

to living rough and fighting a bit," he said.

"But you were young then, Dad!"

"Thanks a lot Phoenix! I'm not ready for burying yet, girl."

"Oh Dad!" cried Phoenix, and burst into tears. Her mother gave Kai a look to freeze boiling water, over the girl's head.

"I'm sorry, Phoenix," Kai said. "Your old dad will be fine. We're too sensible to take risks now, aren't we, Bly?"

Bly looked at him and something passed between them – that flame of fierceness – then Bly noticed me standing on the edge of the light and it was gone.

"Wichapi ... Sacks! I didn't see you there." The sureness was gone out of his voice now he was talking to me. "How are you feeling?" He stepped away from Kai's lantern light and stood close beside me. "Did you see all that?" He tipped his head to the circle, and ran a bony hand over his hair. "I need to explain a bit."

"No, you don't," I said. "I used to think like the old man: Supas and Rebels? I wasn't sure it was my fight. And now I am sure. If you're going to the City, I'm coming."

I was ready to tell him about Nero; ready to say, "I do belong with you, you were right." But Bly looked at me and smiled. "No," he said "No! You can't come."

Remembering now, I can hear the kindness and the fear in his voice, but all I heard then was the "no". He could see I was ready to fight and led me a little way from Phoenix and her family so we couldn't be heard.

"Look," he said, "Manhattan won't be the end of it for me. It's the last Supa City round here, but there are others that need bringing down. Maybe I won't be back at the settlement for a long time."

"Then that's more reason I should come with you!"

"You're too young," he said and put his hand on my shoulder. "You *have* to go to the Rondaks with Nomis and Phoenix."

I snicked my shoulder out from under his hand. "Leaving me behind again! At four old enough to be dumped on a Station. Now I'm too young to come with you?"

"Wichapi..."

"I *told* you not to call me that. You don't know *anything* about me; what I know, what I've seen, what I can *do*! I don't have to do anything you tell me."

He leant down and put his heavy hands on both my shoulders, sure again now, like he was speaking to the crowd. "For your own safety," he said. "Yes, you do."

"Make me!" I turned, too fast for grabbing, and ran.

I didn't have a lantern and everyone was ahead of me or behind. But I was glad to run in the dark and let my anger bleed out into the night. Then an iron grip caught me out of the blackness, and Missouri was beside me, pulling me off the path and between the huts and trees.

"Said I'd come back for you," she said. "Don't want to go to the Rondaks, do you?"

I shook my head and saw her grin gleam white in the shadows.

"Best come along wi' me then!" She dragged me by the arm through the scratching branches. "The river's down 'ere," she said. "Let's go."

"Missouri," I began when I'd got into the canoe. "Can we go to the City?"

She giggled, a sound that was half thrill, half terror, then whispered, so that I wasn't sure who she was talking to, me or herself or someone else altogether. "Yes," she said, "that's where we're going. Bly isn't the only one with work to do, seein' them Supas going down at last!" Then she pushed the canoe out into the water.

I felt it free itself from the bottom and float out, rocking into the deeps, and I wondered again how the river, dark and soft as cloud, could hold us up.

nero

SCURRO hauled me out of the hut after a couple of hours, to explain his plans for the raid on the TV tower. It seemed like he'd got used to us not being related pretty fast. He stood me in the middle of the hangar and looked at me like he looked at his guards or his plane or his weapons: something he needed to use for a while. I thought how he'd used Fortay and me, and found I took to not being his son easily too.

"In three days' time," he said, "you, your Rebels and my guards will take the *Uccello* to the broadcast tower. Murdoch-Sir will be expecting a ceremonial visit from Nabisco leaders. We will be paying our respects, pledging allegiance."

"He'll fall for that?"

"Young Fulton Murdoch is in need of allies. He has already agreed to the meeting. Your people will kill him, overpower his forces and take over the broadcast facility on the 200th floor. You will bind and gag the guards, and leave just in advance of the arrival of Nabisco reinforcements."

Scurro had it all worked out... Weapons, explosives devices, Supas' uniforms, even plans of the broadcast tower. He must have had all this organized for the Rebels Hasp had been going to deliver in the *Uccello*. But the more he talked about how it was all going to work, the more terrified I got. Fortay was the leader, the man of action. I just mended things.

But I didn't have a choice – none of us did. I had to relay the plans to Scanner, Rivet and the rest. I had to train them to carry out Scurro's orders, or we'd all be killed on the spot. The guards watched over us at all times. They listened to every word so there was no way I could modify what Scurro wanted, or tell the Rebels anything that wasn't in his master plan. But all the time, I knew Scurro was lying: there was no way he'd let the Rebels or me out of that Broadcast Tower alive. He needed a pile of bodies to make his deception look good. So all the time I was "training" my Rebel band, I was trying to think of a way we could all escape in one piece.

The good part was that we couldn't practise for the raid tied up, gagged and banged up in a shed. So we were freed to stand around the paper plans of the tower, spread on the hangar floor. Fights and strategies were the Rebels' world, so I thought they should understand Scurro's plans. But it didn't seem to work that way.

"OK, so this is the elevator," I said for the fourth time. "Right?" I pointed to the little box on the paper that showed the position of the lift shaft. "Murdoch will step out through the doors here." A ring of blank, confused faces surrounded me. They didn't seem to get it.

"But it's just a bit of paper, Nero..." said Scanner.

The Supa thugs, detailed to listen to our every word and report to Scurro, found this hilarious. They rattled their loaded guns and cracked all the usual jokes about Worker brain-power. I was almost ready to join in, but I took a deep breath. A very deep breath. "OK, OK. Let's start again."

They were never going to make sense of the plans. How could they, when they'd never been taught to understand any-thing but pictures on a TV screen? I found some chalks and moved around furniture until I'd laid out the floor plan in white lines, chairs and bits of broken aero-craft. I knew how bright the Rebels really were, so I was *sure* they'd get the idea now. But they didn't. It took hours, and every time I started to explain *again*, the guards smirked and whispered. It started to get to me. I kept wanting to yell, "Stop being so *dumb!*"

But the guards' jokes didn't bother the Rebels and at last they did get it, and we could start to work.

"OK. So we come in from here," I said walking between the two chairs that were the doors from the landing platform, next to the ninety-seventh floor. "Me and the two real guards, then Grubber, Spadey and Bead, you'll be in guard's uniforms behind them. Flame, Scanner and Rivet will be dressed as servants carrying the 'gift' for Murdoch."

"Why are they going to let any of us in?" asked Bead,

rubbing his fingers nervously through his beard.

Bead and all the rest too were looking mystified again. What was the matter with them? Had one of the guards slipped some Product into their rations?

"Look," I said, "we don't have time for me to explain. This is just a job we have to do, to stay alive."

"And get Home," Scanner added. I didn't have the heart to say yes or no, or even look at her, but there were nods all round from the Rebels.

"OK," I said, "let's run through it all again. We'll arrive at the TV Station almost at the same time as Murdoch, so there'll be a little confusion to cover us. We'll enter the foyer. They'll come from the west heliport side and we'll come from the east. Murdoch knows Scurro well. He'll accept that, as his son, I've come to show our family's respect, our allegiance. From one family to another. I'll make a little speech. Scanner'll step forward with the 'gift'."

"Then they go into the elevator..." continued Rivet.

"We move back," cut in Bead, "respectful like..."

"And then I hit the detonator!" said Rivet.

"Yep," I said, making the next part nice and clear for the listening guards. "That takes out Murdoch, his bodyguards and the lift shaft, so reinforcements from the lower floors will have to take the staircase." Everybody nodded. At last they'd got it straight, but it had been such hard work!

"After the explosion," I went on, "there'll be a panic.

Nobody will know what's happened. We then have about four minutes to get out. Bead and Spadey, you have to make the Nabisco guards look like the whole thing has been forced on them: tie them up and leave them by the lift. Scanner, Rivet and Flame, you make sure there's no resistance left on that level. Grubber, Spadey and Bead, you secure the stairway."

So far, that was probably how it might really work, but the next part was a lie. "Then we get out before Scurro's reinforcements arrive."

I knew that wouldn't happen. But with the guards watching and listening so carefully, there was no way I could show that, not even in the tone of my voice. I guessed what would actually happen at that point in the plan. Staring down at the chalk lines on the floor, I could see it all unfolding in front of me: Scurro's men would arrive, for sure, but we'd still be there and they'd kill every one of us – probably even their own two guards, to make the whole thing look more authentic.

"Then we all get aboard the *Uccello*," said Scanner, "and Nero takes us to the spacecraft. Easy!" She sounded so bright, so incredibly cheery, that I looked up from the chalk lines at the eagerly nodding heads.

"Easy!" said Rivet, just as brightly as Scanner and a little louder than seemed necessary.

"Yeah!"

"Great!"

"Right!"

Dumb little exclamations of approval sounded all around me. I looked hard at all the faces. They were all smiling the kind of smiles Supas' would *expect* from Workers. Then Grubber said, "Oh, but we mustn't forget how hard 'tis going to be. The fighting and that."

"No," Rivet agreed, "'course not. Serious job." And all the smiles disappeared behind a rash of earnestly folded brows and sternly downcast mouths.

"Oh, yeah. Serious it is."

"Big job. Very big."

"Gonna be tough."

"Yeah."

"Good of your dad to give us this chance really."

Then, with his back to the guards, Grubber winked at me. *Oh*, I thought. *Right. I'm the one who's being stupid here.* The Rebels had been putting on a show, giving their audience of Supa thugs exactly what they expected, so they wouldn't suspect we might alter the plans to suit ourselves!

At the end of every day's "practice" I was locked away separately in an office at the back of the hangar. It was nothing but an airless box, with a cracked concrete floor and walls buckled with damp. I lay on the bare floor all night, dipping into shallow puddles of sleep and thinking. I thought mostly of the part of Scurro's plan where Nabisco reinforcements arrived and blew everyone away. How was I going to get them out of there? And if I did, how was I finally going to tell them about Home? If I got them out alive, whatever followed wasn't going to be wandering in the sunshine and picking fruit off the trees!

I thought too about the letter. I couldn't read it in the pitch-blackness, but I could feel it, tucked inside my clothes, moving up and down with my breathing. I felt its words were written on my skin, and they made me feel a little stronger. *The truth will defeat lies.* Nothing my ex-father had ever told me about Supas, about Workers, about family, had ever been true. Everything about that world was made of lies. And now I hated it all.

At the end of the third night in that office, a tiny line of grey light sneaking along the bottom edge of the door told me the day of the attack on the TV tower had come. I'd watched the blackness all night, waiting for some idea to float out of it and into my head. Something brilliant and ingenious that would save all our skins, and make the non-existence of Planet Home sort of OK for the Rebels. I was just thinking what a waste of time my sleeplessness had been when there was a huge explosion. The whole hangar shuddered, and I heard sections of roof scraping off and clanging to the ground. The line under the door grew red and there were shouting voices and a volley of shots. Then came another two explosions, each followed by a *Wooofff!* which told me they carried a big volume of flame in their wake. The sort of sound a big fuel-bomb makes. The Rebels hadn't been idle, sitting over those four fuel drums every night! A moment later the door blasted open and a singed and grinning Grubber burst in.

"C'mon, Nero, you got to fly that plane of yours."

The hangar was a mass of leaping flame and black smoke, and metal screeched with the heat. We ran through it and out onto the runway, where the *Uccello*'s back showed out of a thick layer of white mist. Two guards were sprawled face down in a spreading pool of blood and there was no sign of anyone else. Next to the smoking hangar Scurro's beloved little pointy plane was in two pieces, like a snapped stick, its long nose bent into the concrete and fires spouting from its ripped middle.

"We could've done a better job on that," said Grubber, "but we needed some fuel to fly with." He grabbed my arm, "No time for gawping. Get inside."

Flame, Spadey and Bead beamed at me as I scrambled through the hold and up to the cockpit, while Grubber got the ramp in and secured the doors. Scanner was circuit checking and Rivet had got the engines fired.

Scanner laughed at my face. "Not such dumb Workers as you thought, eh, Nero?" she said, nudging Rivet out of the pilot's seat.

"Supas are useless at fighting," he said, "but they fixed the *Uccello* all right. Close your mouth, Nero, and get her up there."

I felt the *Uccello*'s pilot seat mould to my back and we raced down the runway and up through the mist and smoke into the dawn sky.

* * *

Everyone was crammed into the cockpit or the corridor beyond, all talking, while I found some clear air above the clouds.

"They never even searched us!" Bead was saying. "They thought as long as we didn't have guns, they were safe."

"Supas just don't know how handy a blade is. Fits in yer boot easy." That was Grubber.

"That's right," Spadey agreed. "I've had a blade in my boot for five years and more."

"So having the blades was part of it, Nero," said Scanner, trying to explain so that I'd understand.

Flame grinned. "And the other part was the guards being so dozy."

"Yeah, and quite liking the look of you, Flame!" added Rivet, and got smacked over the head for it!

"Spadey just sliced the first one before he even woke up..." Bead was talking again, but after that the story became a fast relay, so I never did quite find out who did, or said, what.

"We piped up some fuel."

"Yeah, found a plastic fuel pipe with the cans."

"Set light to the second one..."

"...so he runs off screaming."

"And the third one gets spooked and *he* runs off."

"We rolls a fuel drum into the hangar."

"Nice big bang that made. Finished a couple of Supas, that's for sure."

"So by the time the last Supas is up and ready to fight..."

"...boss man's craft is in bits..."

"...his bully boys are filleted..."

"...his little mate Hasp's either blown to bits or run off..."

"...so anyone who's left legs it!"

"And we spring the coop!"

They all burst out laughing. I shivered, feeling glad I was on the same side as these guys. "Great story, everybody," I said, "but now what do we do?" There was a silence, and for a chilling moment I wondered if their plan was to fillet me too! Then Scanner cleared her throat. Sounded like this was a speech she'd been practising.

"Well," she began, "it's like this Nero." She paused again, and I glanced sideways at her little red face, folded in more than its usual number of creases.

"Go on, Scanner."

"Yeah," said the others. "Go on, Scanner!"

"Well, we thought – I mean, there's Workers still on Stations and we don't know what happened at the settlement. So..." Scanner got slower and slower but it didn't matter because we were back on the talking-relay again, with one voice following another as if they were all thinking together.

"Them Supas. Scurro and that lot, they ain't going to be raising the alarm or anything."

"And we got all the air permits for flying into the City... Found 'em on the panel right here."

"And Fulton Murdoch still thinks you're Nero Nabisco, doesn't he?"

"And we all know the plans."

"And the weapons and explosives is right on board. And the Supas uniforms."

Scanner took up the talking at bullet speed. "We thought we'd go ahead with this raid, with some little changes. Like, take over the TV tower for Rebels and keep Fulton alive 'cos he might be useful. So it ought to work OK."

I guessed they all knew that our chances of success were small and that our chances of getting out again, if we succeeded, were even smaller, but what else were we going to do now?

The flight was bumpy. It took a lot of my attention, which was good, as it helped keep me cool and made the whole thing seem kind of possible. In the few calm minutes I looked over each of the Rebels as they came to be inspected in their Supas' gear. Guards uniforms for Grubber, Spadey and Bead, the long striped tunics of formal servant wear for Flame, Scanner and Rivet. I was the one who looked unconvincing now, still in the ripped remnants of my Blacks under a set of orange overalls.

We came out of the turbulence and I started a nice easy descent towards the City. As we came down the Rebels stared, fascinated, through the cockpit bubble at a city that was nothing like the one they'd seen on TV. No rows of sky-scrapers, shiny with silver, gold and copper, or shimmering with "smart skin" that changed from purple to orange as the day warmed. No glittering roads, full of light and movement. No crystal dome dividing the sky over it all into jewels. It had been fifty years or more since the City had had even a touch of the old glamour of Manhattan.

Our entrance point was the landing platform around Spire 37. I could see its tarnished spike poking out through the smog, like a giant broken tooth. The top fifty stories were missing, blown away in some conflict years ago and, like everything else in the City, never mended or rebuilt. Off in the dirty mist to the left and right, forming a ring of security, were the other spires; blotchy grey now, pitted with holes where bombs and rockets had hit, and missing their pointed tops. All of them had landing platforms halfway up, their sides, impro-vised from concrete and steel girders, looking awkward and frail. Dangling around the spires were the twisted, collapsed remains of the great crystal dome that had once arched over the whole City, keeping out polluted air and toxic rain. The spires had been the supports of the dome, and in places frag-ments of the crystal itself still clung to the wrecked framework, misted and yellowed with smog and neglect.

Beyond the spires were broken skyscrapers in as bad a shape as the spires. Some of them leant at odd angles, or were chopped off where a particularly nasty explosion had blown away a few floors. The better ones had been roughly patched up with dull slabs of concrete, ugly yellow bricks the same colour as smog – even cars, beaten into rough sheets of metal. One of the Murdoch family buildings was entirely faced in old red and blue Chryslers, rolled flat like giant tiles.

Crouched at the foot of the most intact skyscrapers, where the Supas lived, were the Work Houses: roofed-over ruins, blocks built of plastic rubbish and thin concrete, all of them with black guard houses and gun turrets to ensure that Workers only worked *for* Supas and not *against* them. Every morning the Workers would stream out of these miserable little boxes and up into the skyscrapers, to service the Supas' lives. "Look at them all," Scurro used to say, looking down from his study window. "Like lines of dirt."

The ground between the buildings wasn't ground any more. Everything in the City stood in ten floors of trash and water. Generations of rubbish: machines that had broken and been thrown away; buildings that had been blown up. It had filled the roads, the parks and the spaces between everything, along with the rising water from the ocean. The only roads now were Trash Roads, short stretches, built on foundations of crushed garbage or on bridges between buildings. The roads and bridges were made of the same weird mix of stuff that patched the skyscrapers, so that it looked like the trash had just got up and walked, and stuck itself together into some kind of shape. Where several buildings were close together, a platform might be made, enabling craft to come in to land. But competing families regularly destroyed each other's buildings, platforms and 'roads', so, looking across the City, there was almost always something smoking or on fire.

The sharp morning light cut into the smog and showed the City for what it was: ugly, sad and busted. Only Scanner passed any comment on what she saw. "Can't see no space rockets taking of from *this* lot somehow." I didn't dare catch her eye. I brought the *Uccello* down onto the platform around Spire 37, a grimy ring of tarmac and concrete at level one-fifty that ran round the spire like a greasy hat brim, and was supported by a mess of metal girders welded to the floors below.

Everything looked worse than normal. The Ford tower, which might once have been blazing white, had a new hole right through its rust-streaked middle. The hole stared out over the perimeter of spires like an eye socket in a skull. There were fires burning in all the Trash Roads on that side of the City, and nothing was moving anywhere: a sure sign that something bad had happened, or was about to. The buildings downtown were lost in a smear of smog, and somewhere beyond that was the brown, oily ocean and the sun rising over it, regretfully.

Spire platforms were too narrow to allow for proper take-off and landing, so I guided the *Uccello* in vertically. I would have to take off the same way, which used a lot of fuel. I looked at our gauges and winced. I brought her up to the slanting wall of the spire and the rusted metal door of the monitoring station. The huge dark barrel of the monitor cannon was trained on us all the way, swinging round to keep us in its sights. The Air Monitors were the one bit of the Supa system that still sort of worked. All air traffic in or out of the City had to pass between, or over, the spires. Anything without the right papers was either turned away or, more often these days, just blasted into dust.

A slit opened in the metal door and I manoeuvred close enough to open the cockpit porthole right next to it. I took one last look at the papers that Scurro had provided. Had he set us up with dud papers for some complicated reasons of his own? Too late to worry now. I opened the little window beside me and slid the papers into the slit.

While we waited, I put on the dress blacks that Scurro had so thoughtfully provided. Then we waited some more. Everyone was very quiet. Above us, out of our field of vision now, the big cannon creaked to and fro, checking its aim. No sounds came from outside, apart from that small adjusting creak of the cannon. No sirens, no planes, no car noises, not even gunfire. Nothing. As if the City was already dead. *The truth will defeat lies. Stations will lie in ruins, the last City will fall.*

Suddenly there was a loud bleep. A little white light flashed inside the slit and the papers emerged, with the black-cannon symbol of the Air Monitors stamped on the front. I pulled away from the wall of the spire and the cannon came back into view, turning back towards the sky. The *Uccello* took three minutes to get enough power for take off from the spire's hat-brim platform. It was a long three minutes. I watched the cannon the whole time, just waiting for it to twitch and roll back in our direction. It didn't, and soon we were back in the air and on to the next step in the plan.

"OK, Bead, break out these weapons and get everyone tooled up. We'll be landing at the tower in ten minutes. Don't forget, Scanner's staying aboard to keep our escape route covered." I almost sounded like I knew what I was doing. Did they expect me to be a fighter because I was the son of one? I hoped not.

Murdoch's TV tower was downtown. I used to be able to see it from my workshop window, in the Nabisco building on the waterfront. It wasn't pretty, but it was well protected, armoured outside with solid slabs of steel-laced concrete. There was a very well-guarded entrance on the one-fiftieth floor, where a road came in from the car-studded tower next door and connected with five other towers in that part of town, then led down to the Trash Roads on the Low Tens. The Murdochs received private and high-ranking visitors – like us – via a door higher up, at level one-ninety, just ten floors down from all the studios, where the transmitters broadcast TV out to the City and to Worker Stations. There was a small landing platform at that level, snaking round two sides of the building and supported by huge black struts that stuck out from four floors below.

As I brought the *Uccello* round to the east side I saw that

Murdoch had already arrived, his little red craft, almost the same model as my father's, stationed on the platform. We'd have to move fast. He would be waiting for our 'state visit', but he wouldn't wait long. Waiting was risky. Running behind schedule was often a sign that something dangerous had gone wrong.

The moment we were down, I ran below. The "delegation" was lined up, with uniforms on and weapons concealed. "OK?" I said. "Everybody ready?"

I was far from ready myself, but there were nods all round.

Scanner silently shook everyone's hand, but when she got to Rivet he said, "Wait a minute! We haven't decided what we're going to say, on TV, when we take it over."

Scanner smiled at him. "Just say the truth," she replied. "Say it as quick as you can: Supas tell nothin' but lies. There's Product in food to make us stupid. The City's a dump, so get out while you can... And Planet Home is just a big old story to keep us dreaming, not doing. That's right, isn't it, Nero?"

I felt the blood rise to my face and I started to splutter some kind of explanation of my Planet Home promises, but Rivet shut me up. "It don't matter, Nero. We all knows the truth now, so it don't matter what you did before. It's what you're doing next that counts."

I swallowed my heart out of my throat and nodded. We were really, really ready. We stepped down the ramp and set off with the right amount of slow pomp towards the big steel door into the tower. Me out front, Rivet and Flame behind carrying the 'gift' between them on a gold tray. Then Spadey, Bead and Grubber looking good as guards, with one weapon broken and slung over their backs, as was the custom for peaceful meetings like this one, and another loaded and ready under the formal over-shirts.

"What are you going to say?" Rivet asked me out of the corner of his mouth.

"I'm sure something suitable will occur to me." Rivet smiled, and suddenly I felt we might get out of this with our skins.

A slit opened in the steel door. I poked the papers through. But that was only a formality and they came out again immediately. The door clicked and slowly slid open.

We walked inside and behind me I heard little hisses of drawn-in breath. The plans had given us the layout but not the flashy decor. A huge hallway took up all of that level of the building. The floor and walls were of black polished stone, with pools of light here and there from spotlamps in the ceiling. No wonder Scurro was so keen on grabbing Murdoch resources!

Coming towards us across the expensive, old-style flooring was Fulton Murdoch and his little entourage. I took in four servants – apparently unarmed – and two slack-looking guards. I glanced around. The lift shaft and stairway were behind the Murdoch group and to their right. I couldn't see any further signs of Murdoch's people on that floor. Unless there were armed personnel concealed behind panels in the walls, which wasn't impossible, the head of the Murdoch household was almost totally unprotected. It was what we'd expected and yet, seeing it for real, it was weird.

Fulton Murdoch wasn't worried; he was beaming. Whatever line Scurro had spun him, he seemed to be pleased about it. I guessed that any offer of an alliance in such difficult times was pretty attractive. When he got close to us, he stepped away from his people and I stepped away from mine. We stood facing each other in the big shiny space of the hall-way, with our hands crossed on our chests, where they couldn't be up to anything violent. I wanted to spin round and round, and check every empty wall for eyes and guns, but I held myself still and stared hard at Murdoch.

He was a little younger than me. All his senior male relatives had come to nasty and premature ends, and he'd inherited the leadership at thirteen, leaving a whole slew of discontented older cousins to plot against him. Those, I suspected, had become Scurro's new best buddies and were behind today's plot. Fulton was a soft-looking kid, with a fuzz of dark hair over a skull like a light bulb and a wet red mouth. I'd never liked him much, although I knew he was an independent thinker and wouldn't want a bunch of adults behind him pulling the strings. He'd taken on his dad's habit of never dressing in Supas' blacks, but in the tight red plastic jumpsuit that was the family trade-mark. Just like his dad, he looked ridiculous. Actually that helped. How could this little guy in shrink-wrapped polythene be a danger to us? I felt better already.

Fulton stopped smiling. He stood silently, waiting for me to propose whatever it was I was supposed to be proposing. Nothing moved, nobody said anything. I felt sure that at least five extra guards stood behind me, with their barrels pointed at my skull. At last I found something to say. "Murdoch-sir," I started, with a little respectful bow of the head. "We come from Nabisco-sir, my father. We come to offer an assurance of the loyal allegiance of the Nabisco family, that our two clans may unite and be strong in these threatening times."

It was a little general, but I thought quite convincing for this sort of occasion. I clamped my right elbow closer to my body to feel the gun tucked under my clothes, but it wasn't reassuring. It just reminded me that any time now I would have to use it, not to shoot at a target but at people. Any time now there would be real bullets, hitting real bodies, and one of them might be mine. The thought made me feel nauseous so I focused on Murdoch's face again, on the mouth that had started to talk.

"Well, Nero Nabisco, very pretty words, I'm sure!" His voice had broken since I'd seen him last. It was amazingly deep for such a pudgy little kid: rough and raspy, and not at all what you'd expect from his red-packaged frame.

"And sincerely meant, Murdoch-sir."

"Yeah? Well maybe. I understood Nabisco-sir himself was to pay his respects this morning?"

"There has been another Rebel attack on one of our aero-craft. Nabisco-sir sends his deepest apologies."

"He is uninjured, I trust?"

"Absolutely." Knowing Scurro's ability to survive, it was probably true in spite of Bead's efforts with the fuel bombs.

Fulton smiled a tight little formal smile, as friendly as an ounce of plastic explosive. "We need to cement this new-found relationship," he declared. "What if you, Nero, come with me after this meeting? To ensure your father's co-opera-tion in future days." Then he smiled again, like he was inviting me back for a snack after target practice instead of suggesting taking me as a hostage.

Fulton might have looked like an idiot, but he didn't talk like one. His request was utterly outrageous, outside the bounds of any code of Supa behaviour. I was impressed! Power struggles between family leaders happened at a dis-tance – they killed each other's guards and servants, bombed each other's roads and buildings, but never *ever* harmed each other at first hand. That was the etiquette that gave our phony 'delegation' some chance of success. And now Fulton was playing us at our own game.

"I would be happy to come with you," I agreed, with exactly the right amount of solemn concern. "Anything to assure you of the sincerity of Nabisco intentions."

The balloon of tension went flat as fast as it had blown up. Fulton beamed again and snapped his little white fingers over his head. Immediately one of the servants walked forward, hoisting a TV camera to his shoulder and pointing it at us. "I think we should capture this on camera, ready for the City News," Fulton declared.

He liked to feature himself out and about, being a great leader. So nowadays his nightly bulletins were peppered with little clips of him meeting other family leaders; driving his car over repaired bridges; climbing aboard his little red craft.

The servant braced his legs apart, to steady the camera, and switched on. "I'm rolling, Murdoch-sir."

"Good," said Fulton, smiling into the lens, then stepping forward to embrace me.

This was what I'd been waiting for: the moment when I had to be like a Fortay, or maybe a Bly, and make the "little alteration" to Scurro's original plan. For a split second, which seemed more like half an hour, I was leaning over Fulton's shiny red shoulder, looking into the staring black lens of the TV camera. I reached inside my tunic for the gun and shoved it into Fulton's ribs. He didn't struggle, and I guessed violence wasn't a first-hand thing for him either. I jammed the barrel harder against his body than was needed, to stop my arm from shaking. The camera wobbled, but kept recording. The servant was clearly unable to believe what his viewfinder was showing him.

"OK, Fulton," I said, trying hard to control the crazy waver of my voice, "on your knees and face your men."

"Turn that damn thing off," Fulton snarled. The servant

just dropped to the ground, hugging his camera and holding one arm over his head.

Then, from the sickeningly slow crawl of the last minutes, time went into super-acceleration, like a very fast car screeching down a tarmac slope. The Rebels were completely at home. Grubber and Rivet shot, took cover, then shot again. They'd done stuff like this time after time. It was simple. They didn't even think about it.

Grubber opened fire on the Murdoch group. The slack guards went down without getting to their weapons, and the servants ran for the lift. One got a bullet in the leg and fell screaming. The other, Rivet grabbed and knocked out with the butt of the gun as if he were putting a tack in the wall. I didn't see what happened to the last one, but the next time I looked at the stairway his legs were sticking out from behind the wall. They didn't move again.

Three, maybe four seconds after I'd pulled a gun on Fulton, everything was still, apart from the servant who was still screaming. Spadey stood over him and told him to shut up, which he did. I dragged Fulton to his feet and smiled, kind of weakly, at everyone. "Right," I said, "right."

But they didn't hear me. Flame ran to the lift and prised open the doors, her hair streaming out behind her like a red cloud. She threw the gold-wrapped 'gift' down the side of the compartment into the shaft and began to count, one second for every twenty floors. "One ... level one-seventy. Two ... level one-fifty." And as she did so we all ran back to the opposite wall and crouched, ready for the blast coming up the lift shaft. Wherever it exploded, the 'gift' would make the whole lift shaft inoperable, but we wanted an explosion at the level of the main guard house, to reduce any opposition still further. Four ... five ... six.

Flame hit the detonator a beat after six seconds, at about the point when the explosive would be at the security level, on the fiftieth floor. We'd been told that the bomb was just enough to take out a lift shaft and part of the floor, so there would be no damage up as far as the broadcast facility on the two-hundredth. We expected a bang, for sure, with maybe a little vibration as the lift shaft imploded. What we got was a whole lot bigger and I realized I'd never actually checked out the device inside that little gold package.

The explosion was enormous, so loud, that I couldn't say what sort of sound it was, only that it rippled through my whole body and seemed to go on and on and on. I estimated that the amount of explosive in the package was at least four times greater than Scurro had told us it was. While it lasted, the tower shuddered down to its foundations far below the trash and rubble of the Low Tens. A huge crack appeared in the floor at our feet, marble panels fell from the walls, and daylight flooded in as the concrete armouring came off the outside of the building.

When it stopped we were all on the floor, shaken off our

feet. Rivet began to say something, but he was cut off by a huge creaking, groaning sound and suddenly the whole floor lurched and tipped us towards the opposite wall. The lift doors gaped open, perfectly lined up to swallow the cameraman, who was sliding helplessly towards the hole. I grabbed him as he passed me, but my hand closed on the carrying strap of the camera. I reeled it in as I hit the wall just beyond the lift shaft hole, but the man wasn't attached to it any more.

Then everything went horribly quiet. We were lying in a kind of valley, between what had been the marble floor and the wall with the lift shaft in it. There was dust and rubble all over us, and a huge hole above us, where the steel door to the outside had once been.

"Rivet? Grubber? Flame?"

"OK."

"Yeah."

"Still 'ere ... just," said Flame.

"We're OK," called Bead and Spadey.

"Mmmnnnnn!" mumbled Fulton from somewhere by my leg. I rolled away from the wall a little and found him jammed between me and a big lump of armoured concrete, which had somehow fallen without killing anyone. He was furious. "What have you done?" he screamed.

"Pretty obvious, Fulton. Knocked your tower down. Not quite as planned, though."

"So what did you plan?"

"What we planned is pretty irrelevant now."

I got up. Over on the other side of the lift shaft hole, the team were doing the same, brushing the rubble off their bodies and the dust out of their eyes, and cursing. It was plain that Scurro had set us up again. If we'd followed his plan and detonated the device just as Fulton shut the lift doors, this floor and the broadcast floors above would have been in pieces. We'd all have been killed instantly. At least we were alive, but using the TV Station for Rebel purposes was out of the question. The whole tower was collapsing and we had to get out. Another of my great plans had gone down the tubes.

Nobody said anything, but we were all thinking the same thought: what about Scanner and the *Uccello*? Were they both in a thousand pieces below us somewhere, in the trash and ruin of the Low Tens? There was a sudden scraping sound, a loud grinding. I braced myself for a final collapse. How high was one-ninety floors? A thousand feet? Was I going to be killed by the concrete slabs smashing me to pieces on the way down? Or would I last long enough to be smashed to death on the rubble?

But the noise wasn't the tower coming to pieces. It was the *Uccello*, her familiar blunt grey nose having crashed through what had been the wall and was now the ceiling, almost directly above us. For a second I thought she might carry on going and drop straight on top of us. But she didn't. After a little creaking and adjustment she stayed still, as if she'd found a nice comfy perch and was going to stick around for a while.

"Hey," said Rivet, "She's come to get us!"

Scanner's face appeared in the gap beside the hull. "Anybody down there?" she called. We all yelled back. She laughed. "One at a time!"

"Is she damaged Scanner? Could she still fly?"

"I dunno, Nero. Could do. Engines looks all right and that. Hull's in one piece. Wings're OK."

"Can you get us out?"

"I'll drop a bit of rope. Wait on."

Hauling everybody up through what had been Fulton's back door seemed to take hours. The rope kept snagging and the people already out didn't seem to be pulling too hard. I waited until last because that's the kind of stuff that leaders are supposed to do. But as the ruined hallway got emptier and emptier, I got more and more anxious to be out of there. I started to hear sounds from all parts of the building. There were little clicks and creaks, small smashings and cracks from the walls around me. Each one seemed to be the start of the tower dissolving into a pile of dust around me. But I'd seen bombs destroying buildings before so I knew that wasn't the real danger, now the first blast was done. It was the other noise, the quiet one, that was the real trouble. It was a muffled roar, as if a hundred Cadillacs were all revving up together; the sound of fire turning the guts and bones of the building to soup. I reckoned we had maybe twenty minutes before the whole place was just a pool of molten steel and glass. So when the rope dangled down for me, I was really ready to get out.

Grubber's hairy arms lifted me over the twisted metal edge of the doorway and I saw immediately why it had been so difficult to haul people up. I'd imagined the *Uccello* standing on a tilted but intact version of the landing platform, but there was nothing. Nothing at all. The entire landing platform had snapped off. The Rebels, Fulton and his two surviving servants were lined up along the side of the building on a crack in the structure that formed a kind of ledge. Below them was the damaged east face of the tower, stretching in a steep slope down to open space and the long drop to the first trash roads. The only thing saving us was the fact that the *Uccello* was wedged into the side of the building, as if the tower had tried to bite a chunk out of her and stopped with its mouth half-closed.

I straightened up, teetering over the drop, and looked around. The wind had got up and was racing over the surface of the building, whipping hair and clothes and equipment, and bringing fumes and smoke up from the fire below. The Rebels clung on along the little ledge, coughing and holding onto stuff that threatened to blow away. Even Scanner looked defeated, shocked and blank. And bossy little Fulton had an arm over his eyes, blocking out the world. Everyone looked liked they'd kind of given up. It was true that our prospects were not good. I had no idea how to get the *Uccello* free from the tower and there was no other way off. We'd all be fried as the fire reached us, or vaporized when the tower collapsed and dropped us into the inferno. Might as well jump now.

Then I got angry. Really angry. Scurro had known that the bomb would destroy the tower, even if we didn't do exactly as he had planned with it. I'd been stupid enough to let him set us up, just like he'd set up Fortay and me. I wasn't going to die because of him, so that he and the other Supas could fight and kill until all that was left was one little heap of trash, and then fight over that too. No way.

"Get on board," I yelled but nobody moved.

"NOW!" I shouted. "We have no time. The tower's going down. Move!"

The wind blew my voice down the line of Rebels perched on the side of the tower, and they livened up a little, but still they didn't move. This time, without really knowing exactly what I meant, I screamed, "Let's go Home!"

It worked. One by one the Rebels started edging towards the *Uccello*, then up over her wedged-in nose and in through the main door. As they passed me they smiled or nodded, but nobody spoke. Fulton's two injured servants limped aboard last, but Fulton hung back.

"You've been shafted, Fulton," I shouted. "Your cousins hatched this with Scurro. We're the nearest thing you'll ever have to a family again. Get on board!"

He didn't say a word. He just jumped, dived right off, hit the side of the building once and disappeared over the edge into the smoke, like a little red plane.

It's weird how fast you can get used to something. After the first three attempts to get the *Uccello* out of the grip of the tower, I didn't really notice that the cockpit was at forty-five degrees. Rivet in the co-pilot's seat and Scanner under the panel doing running repairs didn't seem bothered by it either. We were all too focused on willing her to wriggle free. The engines seemed fine. They sounded healthy and powerful, but they weren't enough to get her off.

"Now what?" Rivet seemed angry, which was good. It meant he'd stopped giving in. But it didn't mean I had any ideas. "Well?"

"Give me a second! I'm thinking."

"Yeah, right. Thinking."

"I know!" Scanner's little ball face popped up from the panel. "We'll rock her," she said.

"What the—"

"Yeah, Nero, she's right!"

"We get everybody to put all their weight on the untrapped side and lever her out."

I didn't see how it would work but anything – anything – was worth trying. It was getting hotter and hotter, and all we could see outside now was smoke.

When Scanner yelled 'ready', we started the engines. The Rebels and the two injured servants hurled themselves at the port-side hull. Just like before, there was a huge scraping sound and a painful whining as the *Uccello* tried to pull away from the building. She slewed around a little and moved forward, so that for a moment I thought we'd done it, but then she jarred to a stop, still caught. I turned off the engines and right on cue a sheet of flame sliced up in front of us.

Scanner half ran, half fell back into the cockpit. "Why d'you stop?"

"Because we're burning fuel too fast, and when the tower goes down we'll break free, so I want to save some for that!"

"We'll be cinders before that! We have to keep trying!"

"We're already too low on fuel, Scanner. I won't risk another try. It's a waste of time!"

"You'll get us fried!"

I swivelled the chair round to face her, both of us leaning into the starboard side at a crazy angle, both of us shaking with fury and fear. She looked ready to hit me. And I was ready to hit her, small though she was. Down in the hold the Rebels were yelling about something and sounded like they were having another try on their own. Another billow of smoke and flame rolled over the cockpit.

"Oh all right. All right," I gave in. "One more go."

Just as I said it, the *Uccello* lurched. Everything that had slanted was suddenly straight and a whole load of what I guessed were concrete fragments hit the outside of the hull. Something smashed into the cockpit window and cracked it. Everybody was yelling: me at Rivet, Rivet at the controls, Scanner at the guys in the hold, and all of them at each other and back at her. The Cadillac roar multiplied a thousandfold and a whole load of different flame colours – red, yellow, green and blue – leapt over the cockpit bubble. I couldn't tell what the engines were doing because the sound outside was so loud, it drowned them. Dust and smoke and flame poured around us, and I felt the craft start to fall with the tower. I pushed the throttle right up to the limit and pulled back, to take her nose up as straight as it would go. Nothing happened. She carried on going down, still held by the dying building. And then there was the tiniest of judders, really dainty, and my little bird shot upwards, free! I thought we might go slap into something I hadn't seen in the smoke, but I aimed her as vertically as I could. Suddenly there was clearer sky and down below us a cloud of dust rose where the TV tower had been.

But we weren't even starting to be out of trouble. "The engine on this side's on fire!" Flame's voice carried from the starboard porthole in the hold. Right on cue a missile scraped our nose.

"What was that?!" said Rivet.

"Air Control. We're flying without papers, and the TV

tower's just been blown up. They're a little jumpy. We have to get down, between the buildings."

Below us, just visible through the wreckage of the TV tower, was the Trash Road called the Bowery, which ran between the two least damaged sections of the City: Greenwich on one side and Alphabet Town on the other. I dropped the *Uccello* into the dust, where the Air Controllers couldn't find her, and headed for the Bowery Mouth, the narrow opening into the long road that led all the way downtown.

Rivet saw where I was heading and yelled, 'We can't fly in a space that small!"

"We don't have much choice, Rivet," I replied.

As fast as I'd taken her up from the tower, I took her over the square next to the Murdoch building next door. No missiles followed and there was still nothing out on the streets. Odd, but good for us. There was an open space after the Murdoch building, where a big bomb had gone wrong ten years ago and taken out almost half a block. I slowed down as we crossed it and aimed at the black slit between two solid lines of scrapers.

"It's too narrow, Nero."

"No, it's not. The *Uccello* is ten metres from tip to tip. The Bowery is fifteen metres most of the way. That gives me a five metre space for mistakes. Anyway, I've done it before." It was partly true. The *Uccello was* ten metres from tip to tip.

The Greenwich and Alphabet buildings on either side of

the Bowery were mostly accommodation for Supa guards and minor Supa families. The buildings were missing their top floors, but the fifties to the hundreds were intact and densely occupied, with little home-made bridges at around the thirtieth floor level. Nobody would follow us because it was too narrow, and Air Control wouldn't fire down there because stray missiles could be embarrassing. I flew my bird down, so she was almost skimming the trash layer. I could see the glint of dirty water in old window spaces, and hear the *drub, drub, drub* of her engines as their revving bounced off the walls either side. The flimsy little bridges flashed past above us, ahead and then gone, ahead and then gone. Mostly it was all a blur of lit windows, dark windows, windows with faces in, bridges with people on and empty bridges, and the endless rusty surface of the trash. We shot from the end of the Bowery, with the buildings flashing by faster and faster, like the film of the old guy and the buffalo when I wound it too fast. I took the bird even lower and wove between the sad rows of Work Houses down on the Battery. Just before we reached the bay, where we could crash-land on the water hidden in smog, in the last window of the last House I saw, clear as a frozen frame of film, a tall, dark-skinned woman with a baby in each of her bent arms.

It was totally black. I felt as if I was upside down, but how could that be? Then I remembered hitting the water. We must have flipped. My legs were caught under the pilot's seat and I was dangling down into the cockpit roof. I had a lump like a fist on the back of my head and sticky stuff I guessed was blood on my face. Below me I could hear something moving a little. "Rivet? Scanner?" I called. There was no reply, but I wasn't certain I'd made any sound. Maybe my voice didn't work in this darkness. I reached up and put my arms around the seat, so I could free my legs and drop down, the right way up. It took a while.

Standing on the floor, I felt better. Except that it was wet. The *Uccello* had managed to float but she was leaking and would sink. I had to get everyone out before that happened. I groped around on the floor that had been the ceiling. I found a foot, then a leg and then the rest of Rivet. He was breathing! I sat him up against the wall to keep him from drowning while I looked for the others. Scanner was in the cockpit passage, wedged on her head with her body and legs up the wall. I found her because I fell over her. I put her the right way up. She felt horribly limp, but she whimpered when I moved her so I knew she was alive. I slid down into the water there and breathed for a few minutes, feeling the relief that Scanner and Rivet were still alive.

I fumbled towards the hold. The wrong way up and in darkness, my old familiar *Uccello* wasn't so familiar any more. The cockpit corridor seemed to go on for too long. I banged into the aft wall of the hold before I realized I'd walked the length of the ship. "Anybody there?" I said. There was a kind of groan. "Who is it? Where are you?"

"Here!" It sounded like Bead. He was wandering in the dark too and we collided over a heap of people.

Everyone who'd been in the hold had been crushed into a single pile by the impact. At the bottom was Spadey. He could move and talk. When we'd helped him work free, we carefully checked the people above him. We found a pulse in two: Flame and the younger of Fulton's servants, the one with the leg wound. I found Grubber by his arms and beard, and held his wrists for ages, hoping to feel some life, but there was nothing. I checked him over with my hands and found that the top of his head was sort of mushy. I was glad there wasn't any light to see by.

We had to find the rear cargo doors, now somewhere above us in the 'ceiling'. Bead managed to put me on his shoulders and I tied my belt to the inner handle so we could locate it again in the dark. Then gradually we moved the injured survivors into position underneath. We had to rest after every effort, and one or other of us would pass out for minutes on end. The bubble of air trapped in the *Uccello*'s hull had saved us from drowning, but now it was slowly suffocating us. When we finished moving everyone into position, ready to get out, we both sat down in the water, unable to do any more. The effort of reaching the doors and getting them open was just too much.

The sound of tapping woke me up. A tapping along the outside of the hull. It moved all the way along, from the stern to the cockpit and back again. There were whispers too, and then scraping and scrabbling right above our heads. They were just sounds. I wanted the sounds to go away so I could drift back to wherever I'd been. But they didn't, and the gentle taps turned to loud bangs. Suddenly I knew what it all meant: someone had come in a boat, inspected the whole craft, and was now breaking open the cargo doors.

It had been around eleven in the morning when we'd flown down the Bowery. Now it was pitch-dark. Blackness and smog swirled together around two heads of white hair and the tiny stick-light that lit them. Our rescuers looked old and skinny, but they were as strong as steel. They hauled us all out – even Bead – and laid us on the *Uccello*'s hull. We glugged down fresh air, coughing away the unconsciousness that had nearly finished us.

"You the ones who took out the TV tower?" one of the boatmen asked, cackling madly before he got a reply.

"What's it to you?" Scanner was already back on form!

"Nothin'. Just we heard the TV tower had gone down."

"And that's not all..." said the second boatman, and they laughed together again. "Looks like the whole City's going down."

I opened my eyes. It was incredibly dark. There were no stars, and the reflection of the City's lights, which normally bounced off the clouds on starless nights, was faint and reddish. I lifted my head and looked all around. There was a little glitter on the water, which showed up the survivors laid on the hull. Beyond that, where skyscrapers should have been picked out in lights, was nothing. Just a bright line of flame on what must have been the water's edge. "Where's the City?" I asked. "Where are we?"

"Out in the bay," said one of the little guys. "The bottom of Bowery's just over there, like always."

"Like I said, there's a lot more going down than the TV tower," his friend repeated, and the two of them sniggered again.

Before I could ask any more, there was a huge explosion. One of the buildings to the west of central – a Ford family place – lit up in flame and sent long fingers of light and fire up into the sky. At the same moment all the lights in the Nabisco building – my old home on the waterfront – came on, and the vast TV screen taking up a quarter of its south side flickered alive. Half a mile away, across the black water, Scurro's face blazed out of the night. Not only alive but in command of a broadcast facility! He was going to be the last breathing rat on the trash heap!

But whatever Scurro had planned didn't work out: he managed just ten words, which bellowed out across the water and must have echoed up the long, empty streets. "Fellow Supas, we are living in difficult times. I am—"

Then there was another explosion and the top of the Nabisco building burst into orange flame. Scurro's grave face sank back into the blackness, in a shower of sparks. I thought it was appropriate that his last words to his world were 'I am'. It had always been a kind of motto for him, I guess.

"Ain't safe to be 'ere," the first boatman said, his face in the small light all angles of fear. "That fuel dump on the shore, leaking onto the water. All the surface'll burn, I reckon."

"Yeah," added the other. "We needs to move on. You want to ride to the far shore?"

I looked at the boat. It wasn't much more than a kind of upturned hat, but once again we were without a lot of choices. "How many can you take?"

The two guys looked at each other, but didn't speak. Between them they didn't seem to need talking; only a long, high laughing that set your teeth on edge. "Can't take you all. One'll have to stay."

One'll have to stay? Which one? Fulton's servant, because he's ill and we don't know him? Bead or Spadey, because they're big and tough? Flame, because she's been stupid enough to fall for Hasp's lies? Rivet, because he would if I asked him? Scanner – well, there wasn't even the smallest reason to think it could be her. No, it had to be me. *What did you think?* I asked myself. *That you were going to get to play happy families with Rivet and Scanner? Nero, you are pathetic.*

"But there's only six of us!" said Scanner.

"Five's all. We'll sink with six."

"Can't we come back for the one who's left?" pleaded Bead.

"No, too dangerous," said the boatmen together.

"We can't leave anyone," Scanner insisted.

"Right then..." The two boatmen started getting into their boat.

"Wait just a second," I stepped in. "We need to talk about this."

The boatmen looked at me as if that was an idea beyond their comprehension. "Be quick."

Everybody started offering to be the one who stayed – even Fulton's servant, which was pretty sweet, I thought.

"Shut up, all of you shut up. You've all heard of my dad, Bly, right?" *Huh more than I have,* I thought.

They nodded.

"Some kind of big famous Rebel leader, right?"

They nodded again.

"So if the City's going down, he *has* to be here somewhere, right?"

"Right."

"So he'll come get me."

There was no response to that.

"And even if he doesn't, I'm his son, so you have to do what I say. Get off this craft NOW!"

Nobody moved. The boatmen were getting nervous and the

Uccello was sinking ever lower in the water. I got desperate. "Back at the settlement I lied to you. I told you I was on your side and I wasn't. All the time I was going to take you to the Supas." Scanner told me to shut up and started crying, but I kept on and on. "I lied to you about Planet Home, remember?" I yelled. "I've lied all along. I'm just a Supa. Leave me!"

Spadey stopped me. Punched me neatly in the belly, so I was winded and couldn't talk. "That's enough, Nero," he said. "You're one of us. And you know it."

"Yeah," I wheezed. "Yeah. That's why you *have* to get in the boat…"

For a moment everything froze. Then Scanner nodded.

"C'mon, Flame, let's get these lads sorted," she said. Quietly they all got in the upturned hat. Nobody said anything, not even goodbye. I pushed the little boat away from the *Uccello* and it was instantly swallowed by the dark and smog and smoke. They were safe. At last I'd got something right. I lay down on the wet belly of my dear dead bird and cried myself into nothingness.

sacks

MISSOURI kept paddling all night. One side then the other, one side then the other. Never fast. Never slow. Never stopping. I paddled too. Badly at first, not keeping to her pattern. But then I got used to the strength of the water, how its softness turned hard and could snatch the paddle away, and I fell in with her. One side then the other, one side then the other. On and on, until all there was in the night was the dark itself and a hurt in my shoulders the size of the world. If I slowed, or missed a stroke, Missouri said, "You want to get to the City fast? You paddle!"

Far into the night, rain began to fall. I didn't fear it as being toxic any more, but I felt its cold, running down my back, stealing all the warmth of my body. My arms began to shake with it, so my paddle rattled the side of the canoe with every stroke. After a long, long time the rain stopped and shapes began to show in the dark: Missouri, swinging from one side to the other, and the line of the canoe in the water.

Grey-blue light came out of the air, making the surface of the river and the high banks and the trees out of itself. Sky, earth, river and us, one thing in the darkness, split apart again in the light.

"You've learnt paddling," said Missouri. "Now there's other stuff to learn."

She turned the canoe across the river, easily and lightly. It came to rest with a little sigh on a mudbank under the branches of the biggest trees I'd ever seen. We got out onto the mud and pulled the canoe up the bank. All I could think of was lying down right there on the wet ground and sleeping for ever. But Missouri pulled me to my feet the moment I sat.

"Why aren't you tired?" I almost whimpered.

"I ain't never tired. I never been tired in all my long life."

"I'm tired."

"Your body ain't tired. 'Tis your spirit that's tired."

"What's a spirit?"

"You don't know, I can't tell you. Anyway, if you're asking me things, then you ain't tired! No time for talking now. C'mon. We got food to catch."

She handed me a blade. It had a smooth handle and a flat pointed metal part that gleamed in the dull light. "That's yours. Keep it in this." She passed me a sort of blade-shaped bag on a string, to hang around my neck. "Don't cut yourself!"

Then she set off, up the shadowy bank where there was hardly enough light to know where your feet were, and in among the trees. She moved fast, with a kind of roll, but she made no sound. I snapped and crashed with every step, until she turned to tell me, "Put your feet just where I put mine. Follow in my steps with your feet. You'll move quiet enough then." It was hard to do. She moved so quickly, I had to look carefully to spot where her feet went. What's more, her legs were a good deal longer than mine. But I soon got the idea, if I managed to do just as she told me, I didn't need to look where I was going.

On and on we went. My heart pounded so loudly, I thought it must be drumming outside my body. I forgot the pain in my shoulders and the chill in my bones as it was replaced by the ache of my legs. Just as I thought I couldn't follow another one of her swinging strides, she stopped, bent at the knees and sat on her ankles. I wasn't so fast, but I did it too. Missouri was staring straight ahead, though I couldn't see at what. So I looked around, grateful to be still.

In the time we'd been walking, the grey light had turned to yellow and it found its way under the trees. It came between the great trunks in long lines; and when the wind made the tops of the trees move, it cut under the branches and squeezed past every twig in bright flashes. Even the leaves couldn't keep it out. It shone right through them, or fell between them in little round splodges onto the ground. And wherever it touched, it showed colours; so many different greens that I wondered why we had just one name for them.

Missouri shifted a little, and I felt her wide rear brush my arm. And then she was gone. The silence was gone too. I was in the middle of great noise – breaking of branches, heaving of breath and a sort of scream. I stood up and saw her, tangled in leaves and greenery ten feet away, the raccoon tails flying around her like a wind, and a big, brown struggling creature wriggling under her great body. "Come here!" she shouted.

She'd got the creature to the ground and was sitting on its back, her legs round its body, one arm round its neck and another holding its head. Its big eyes rolled around, frightened, looking for a way to escape, but there was none that I could see, with that weight on top of it. Even with its skinny little legs folded under and its head bent back, the creature was beautiful, like the cranes. Its body was covered in short thick hairs, cream on the belly and brown, like the colour of my own skin, on the rest. Its ears were shaped like long leaves and its snout was smoothed out, as if a hand had stroked it into being. Missouri put her blade to the creature's throat and cut.

"No!" I cried out. "Don't!"

But it was too late. Hot blood, the colour of my own, the colour of the crane's blood, rushed out. There was so much of it. It ran everywhere, making the smooth brown and white hair all red and sticky. The big eyes looked at me still, but now the dark inside them was blank. Missouri fixed me with a long and steady gaze. "You live on this Earth, girl," she said, "and killing's part of it. You want to eat? Then we got to eat this deer. If we don't, there's no hope of getting to the City and having the strength to do what needs doing."

"Can't we eat something else?"

"Nothing else *to* eat out here. No corn. No Meals! You want to go back? Go up to the Rondaks with the mothers and their babies. That what you want?"

"No."

"Good. Then help me with this."

I thought of Nero, somewhere in the City. And I thought of the pictures on the rocks – the people and the animals, eating, being eaten, and going on together all the same – and I helped Missouri carry the deer to the river.

On the clean stones of the bank she cut up the body. I tried to blur my eyes so as not to see any more blood. But it seemed the bloody part was all done, and I found my eyes wouldn't blur. Missouri worked so skilfully, her big body seeming small and agile as she moved around the deer. First she removed the skin with the hair, called fur. It came off clean in one piece, like overalls pulled off a person. Underneath, the deer was so ordered, with lines and blocks of red flesh that Missouri said were muscles. "That's what moves it. That's the part we mostly eat." Lying on the ground without its fur, its four legs stretched out, the deer made me think of a person, curled asleep with arms and legs on one side.

Then she split its round belly and ran her knife up the middle of its chest, like a long zip, to show what was inside. It was more than beautiful. I'd never seen any working thing that looked so good. Mott's machines were never so well kept! It was a marvel. Missouri showed and named every part. The guts, all piped and folded, the big flat liver lying under the ribs, the heart, the lungs. So many different parts, all soft, but shaped so cleverly and packed neatly to fit exactly in the space. I touched and felt everything. The lungs I liked especially, each one bigger than my two hands but as light and soft as touching air. I thought of the white clouds I'd seen from the *Uccello*. "Tis full of a million little sacs," Missouri told me, "to catch the air and put it in the deer's blood." And the heart I liked too. Missouri cut it open to show the chambers inside, with their smooth, shiny walls and the valves that kept the blood from flowing the wrong way. I could feel the strength of it, its springy pump that worked and worked all the days and hours and seconds of a whole life. Like Missouri, never tired.

"All animals is made the same," Missouri explained. "Deer, raccoon, squirrel, bird, human is all the same inside their skin – guts, liver, lungs and heart." I put my hand on my own chest to feel the beating there. I smiled to think of the blood pushed by the walls and directed by the little cups of gristle, just like the deer's heart, just like the crane's.

We walked back to the canoe with four legs of deer. Missouri made a fire and slung the legs above it, turning them over the flames. They browned and sizzled until they smelled like food. We ate one all up, until our bellies were tight. I picked the last bits of meat off the pale, hard bone, then felt my own arm and the bone inside the flesh, like the deer's foreleg. Then Missouri rubbed hot ash from the fire on the inside of the deer's skin. "There's no time to cure it proper, but that'll make a start," she said. "You'll have something to keep out some cold."

I don't know when I fell asleep, but when I woke up I was in the bottom of the canoe, with the deer's skin wrapping my body like my own coat of fur. Missouri didn't tell me to row, so I fell asleep again. Her paddle woke me, shoving into my stomach and poking me awake. It was night, but not dark. Light from a fat white moon lit the sky and fell in streaks and blobs on the broad river. It showed the outline of high wooded banks on either side of us. I sat up and reached for my own paddle, and began. One side then the other. One side then the other. The moment I'd got the rhythm, Missouri started asking questions, as if she'd been waiting all the time I'd slept.

"You ever been in the City?"

I didn't answer.

"You ain't, have you?" She gave that laugh that made my hair stand up. "I'll have to guide you then."

"How do you know the City, Missouri?"

"I was a Worker there long ago. Taken by the Supas when I was a little one. But I got away! And I've been going back, quiet, slipping in and out to see what's happening, preparing for when the Supas is all gone, all the years since. Paddle hard, we need to cross to the Sound by morning."

I didn't know what she was talking about, but I didn't have the breath for more talk. The banks of the river dropped away, until we were paddling the dark band of water in a flat white landscape that stretched all around. I'd felt safe paddling in the shadow, with the river at the bottom, a long, safe cleft in the world. But now it seemed the river was higher than the land, standing out for miles around. I ducked a little in the canoe, but Missouri sat as tall as ever, paddling as constantly as a heart. I didn't see why she wasn't afraid that unfriendly eyes might see us.

We rounded a long bend and I saw that ahead the river disappeared. The strange, pale ground just ate it, and it wasn't there any more. Missouri steered us towards the bank and the canoe made a crunch as we ran aground on a beach that gleamed white in the moonlight. We stepped out onto the sloped bank and I saw what made it white: the land from one horizon to another was made of bones. The river was flowing through a hill of them; more bones than stars in the sky.

"There's all sorts in 'ere," said Missouri, and pointed to a bone shaped like a bowl with a round handle. "Most be human, like that. See, that's the head top and there's where the eye was. But there's some others too. Bones of animals I ain't never seen before…"

"There's so many!"

"There was so many things alive before the Supas killed

'em. They put the bones 'ere, then dropped mines all among 'em, to guard the crossing to the Sound. You walk on this lot –" Missouri stamped on the bones under her feet – "and you'll be blasted, sure."

"Where're we going then?"

"Over this, of course." She stamped again and began to pull the canoe up the white bank. "The Supas needs a place to land their craft if there's trouble out on the bones, so they left a gap, right across, with no mines! I'm the one that knows it. Missouri's own pathway!"

We lifted the canoe onto our shoulders and began to walk. The bones crunched under our feet and I looked down to see whose remains I might be hurting. In the bright moonlight I could see shapes and sizes as clear as day. Many were just fragments, rods of white with broken ends, or flat pieces smashed from head bones. But there were whole bones too: tiny skulls smaller than my hand, and huge ones that we had to step over. Missouri had a word for some of them – "raccoon", "rat", "human", "fox", "eagle" – but not for all. I reckoned there were fifty different kinds of head bones there, all different shapes and sizes; long jaws and short, pointed teeth and flat. But no matter what the shape and size, they all seemed to be made to the same pattern. On each one I could see where the eyes had looked out on the same world .

Back along the line of the river, now in the distance, I could make out hills, and right in front of me all I could see was Missouri's head. But in every other direction there was only the whiteness of the bones. If they stretched for twenty miles all around and were thick enough to bury a river, how many bodies did that make? The thought of so much death kept my mind off the canoe digging in my shoulder, and stopped me wishing for Missouri to get tired and rest. I didn't want my bones added to this great pile, so, though my legs hurt, I was glad of her fast pace. All I wanted was for our journey across the bones to be over and done with. Every moment I wished I could run, not walk. And then Missouri stopped. She put down the canoe without a word and stood staring.

"What is it?" I asked.

"Hush!"

I hushed and tried to listen through the blood rushing in my head.

Tchk, tchk, tchk. Small footsteps chinking on the bone! I looked towards the sound and saw a creature with a pointed face, four little legs and a fat tail, rushing over the white bone-field to our left. It was close enough to see the shine of its eye catch the moonlight.

"Get down!" whispered Missouri, "Fast!"

I threw myself flat, and the moment I pressed my face into the jumble of white shapes, the bones pushed back. A little ripple at first, then a huge punch as the whole mound of them seemed to jump upwards, and the air cracked with a bang loud enough to call the Supas back from Home. I opened my eyes and looked out from under the shelter of my arm to see a rain of bones falling all around. When it stopped I sat up. The canoe was covered in little rips and holes. Missouri was patting it with her hand and cursing. I thought perhaps the bang had made her madder than ever, and that I'd have to try and find my path to the City all alone. A cold lump of fear rose in my chest at the thought. But as quickly as she'd begun to fuss over her broken canoe, she stopped. "Dig!" she said. "Dig fast! We got to bury it and us. The Supas'll be 'ere to check that bang pretty soon."

The bones were dry and easy to scoop up. We had the canoe out of sight pretty quickly, and then we buried ourselves under just enough bone to hide us. We lay side by side, our heads together looking out through the smashed side of a huge skull that Missouri couldn't name. On one side of the sky, the moon had got big and yellow, and dropped down to meet the earth. On the other side, the sun was taking the dark out of the air as it moved up, ready to rise. All I could hear at first was our breathing rasping against the bits of bone around our faces. Then I began to hear the craft coming, and soon I saw its light.

I'd never seen such a craft before. It was a bubble with a tail sticking out of the back and a ring of fast-sweeping blades on top. It had two legs and on the end of them, great flat feet. It moved fast, and in a moment the sound and the bright light were all round us. I peered through the window of bone and I could see they were landing almost on our heads!

"They ain't seen us." Missouri spoke loudly over the noise of the craft she called a 'chopper'. "Stay still!" The engine noise died and we were covered by black shadow. The belly of the chopper was right over us, its huge, flat landing feet either side. Its lights shone out in front of it, showing the big hole where the little creature had run, and found a mine. Two Supa guards got out. I saw their boots in the light and heard their voices. They weren't keen to get close to the hole, but just stood by the landing feet and surveyed the area.

"How dense are the mines on this section?" said one.

"The landing line is clear of them for two metres either side of here." That was Missouri's own pathway!

"I know that. Out there, I mean. Where the hole is."

There was a crackle of paper. The guard was consulting a plan. "Out there? One every ten inches east to west, and one every twenty north to south."

"So that crater's probably taken out a whole twenty-metre section. We could walk in and take a look."

"No point taking the risk. There's nothing I can see."

"So what do we do?"

"Follow orders. Replace any exploded mines and close up the landing gap all the way along."

"There'll be no safe landing if we do that!"

"I don't make the orders. I just do as I'm told. The way things are with the Rebels right now, we don't want any gaps in the City defences."

"Yeah, you're right. Let's get back up. We got enough mines on board to do this now?"

"Yep. We can have the whole strip carpeted in two hours. Be back at base in time to get your belly filled!"

The guards got back into the chopper and as soon as the engine noise began again, Missouri wriggled out of her bone cover. "They're closing up the path. If we stay 'ere we'll be stuck, with mines all around. Might even get one on the 'ead, the way they drops 'em! Get on that landing foot! I'll be on t'other. We'll take a ride with the guards!"

There was no time to ask questions. But I knew she was right, so I half crawled, half scrambled towards the foot of the chopper. It was hollow metal, like a big dish. I reached and pulled myself over the lip, and caught sight of Missouri doing the same on the other side. The chopper lurched and started to tip me about. I grabbed the solid metal upright strut that held the foot to the belly of the craft, and felt us leave the ground. The air rushed over my back, ripping at my clothes. I put my head down and shut my eyes.

The chopper flew up and down the length of Missouri's pathway three times, so low I could hear the sound of the blades bouncing off the bone-covered ground. Then, at last, I felt it rise and turn, and begin to move more quickly. The guards were heading back to wherever they came from and once they landed we'd be pretty easy to spot. I raised my head a little and looked around as much as I could, while hanging onto the strut and having my eyes blown out by the wind. The front quarter of the foot was covered, like the front part of a shoe, and under it, just a second's crawl from where I clung, was nice safe darkness. I'd make for that the moment the feet touched the ground, and hope that no one saw me first.

No one did see me, though it was full light when we landed. I lay in my hiding place under the cover, almost too scared to breathe or blink. We were near the City, I guessed, but nothing I could see told me how close or how far I might be from finding Nero. Between the lip of the foot I lay in and the belly of the chopper was a strip of tarmac and sky. I stared out at the little patch of world visible to me, waiting every second for a Supa's face to appear in that space and direct a bullet into my head. But it didn't happen. Instead, I saw craft passing in the sky at a distance and heard footsteps and voices, but nothing close or threatening. After a long while, I found the nerve to whisper to Missouri, but as loud as I dared was probably still too quiet for her to hear me as she lay in the other foot. There was no reply anyway. So I stayed still and waited some more.

I must have fallen asleep when suddenly a shot woke me. Behind me, away from my bit of sky and landing strip, a fight was happening. There were shouts, more shots, explosions and then nothing. Just the light changing in the sky, and the shadow of the chopper getting longer and deeper on the tarmac. I knew that when it was dark I'd have to crawl from my foot and find out where I was, and what I could do next. But as the dark came down I began to hear footsteps in my own breath, and feel eyes searching and waiting in the shadow outside. So it was long after the sky and the ground had merged in the black that I crawled, little by little, out of hiding.

First I crossed to the other foot. "Missouri?" I hardly more than breathed it, but in the quiet that had settled, like a sort of dust, she would have heard. There was no reply. I got on her foot and crawled about, but she wasn't there. I lay in the lip for a while, thinking. The City was somewhere out in the dark, and somewhere in that darkness was Nero. Where would I start to look with no Missouri to guide me? It was worse than stepping out onto the prairie, or dangling from the *Uccello*. How would I do it? Then old Mott spoke up inside me, as if all I'd done was drag my feet on the way to the Unit sheds. *No good lying there, that's sure!* he said.

Slowly and quietly, I got out onto the tarmac and began to move towards the dim shape of a square building a few hundred metres away, every step feeling as loud as a shot. The Supas' markings on the tarmac – arrows, words and such – swam at me, white in the gloom, like figures in the dark. More than once I fell flat to the ground because of them.

Close to the building I began to see its shape and catch a little shine from the glass of doors and a few windows high up. It was low – two small storeys – with a tower at one end. I put my hand on a glass wall and guided myself along it until a gap and broken shards under my feet showed where a whole huge pane had been blasted out. The shock of the scrunching glass fragments under my feet made me freeze. I looked down. A dark shape was on the ground, big and lumpen. It took a minute to see it was a human – a body – lying quite still. I pushed it with my foot and it rolled so that a pale patch of face showed in the dark. I reached down and touched the neck: it was cool and there was no pulse.

I stepped over the body, trying to keep steady, and went into the building. It was hot inside and there was a smell, not one I could name, but bad. Patches of dim light showed through a glass wall on the other side of the room so I could see it was a big space, almost like the hangar of Station 27. I stood looking, working out what the small reddish gleam was showing me: eight bodies on the shiny floor, more broken glass, and two doors next to each other behind a kind of console. One was closed, the other stood half open, as if someone had rushed through it. From what I could see, the bodies wore guard gear. *I should check them for weapons,* I told myself, *maybe get myself a gun.* But I didn't. I stood listening for breath, for movement somewhere in the building, but there was nothing. At last, I crossed the hall space to where the main door had been smashed wide open.

I'd passed right through the building now and I could see where the dim light was coming from, without layers of darkened glass wall to blur it. In front of me, on the other side of a body of water that lapped somewhere close below, was the City. All my life I'd seen pictures of it on TV – the shining towers under the big glittering dome. Even at night the towers shone with lights that danced off the arc of the dome and lit the water at the end of the streets. But, like everything the Supas showed on TV, that wasn't the truth. What I saw were towers, broken and bent; dark shapes against the naked sky, with no dome to keep out the touch of rain. A few dots of yellow light glimmered here and there, but the main light was from fires that ran along the edge of the water at the far side and leapt up inside some of the buildings, showing their shapes, clear and red. A little breeze brought some ragged snips of sound to me: voices shouting, shots and a faint crackle of fire.

It was true what they'd said. The Supas were on the way down; their City wasn't their own any more. It seemed more like something of ours, small and worn out. Finding Nero didn't seem so impossible after all.

I had to get a boat. It was the only way to cross to the City. Supas used boats – I'd seen them in the TV pictures of the City – and if this place had been full of guards then they must have had boats to keep watch on the water. I moved forward in the dark, towards the sound of lapping water, and came to the edge of a high wall that dropped from my feet, straight to the water below. I peered down. I could make out dim shapes moving and hear a hollow knocking as one shape knocked against the other. Boats! I moved as fast as I dared along the wall edge until I came to steps leading down. They were wet and slippery and I trod extra slowly.

The shadow at the bottom was deep black, but the water caught the far gleam of the burning City and bounced it here and there to show a prow, a stern, a curving side. There were many small boats tied up along a walkway and there was enough noise – the knock of the boats against each other and the rattle of their gear – to cover me as I felt my way around. I was still slow and frightened, checking all around me every second and crouching down in the darkest shadows at any sign of danger – a flash of reflected light that seemed like a moving body, a creak that might be a footstep. I climbed aboard small craft, looking for the right one, something that somehow reminded me of the canoe I'd grown used to. But they were all complicated things, full of engines and such. What was more, they were all wet, with water to the knees in every one. I didn't know much about boats, but I was sure they were meant to be dry on the inside. I guessed the Rebels, or whoever else had killed the guards lying in the building, had holed the boats to make sure there were no easy getaways.

I'd checked all along three sides of the quay and just found water in the bottom of the last boat tied up there when I caught a flicker of movement from the side of my eye. I crouched low, tucked my head down behind the side of the boat, and backed slowly to where a mass of ropes and metal parts would blur my shape. I looked again to where I'd seen the movement and from the end of the quay came voices, and the sound of splashing. A small craft, so small and so low in the water that it was hard to see, slid to the end of the walkway, moved by a couple of paddles, like Missouri's canoe. *Perfect*, I thought. The voices were hushed now, quieted out of the same caution as I felt, I guessed. In the blackness under the shadow of the walls, I thought I could see figures getting out of the little craft. *My* craft, my route to the City! I had to get it.

I climbed over the side of the half-sunken boat I was on and let myself into the water. I didn't expect the cold, and I could have yelled as it got under my clothes. I kept low in the water, with just my eyes above the surface and my nose every little while for a breath. As I pulled myself along the edge of the walkway towards the craft, I could hear the water slapping its sides close to my head. If I reached up, the rope holding it to shore would be there, ready for cutting. I'd push the craft from the walkway and pull myself aboard when it was out of reach of any hands grabbing for it in the dark. In my head I was already paddling across the water to the burning towers of the City.

But as I got my fingertips on the rope it was jerked upwards. There were screams and shouts and sounds of a struggle. I reckoned someone else was trying to take my craft. I wasn't going to let it happen so I pulled myself up on the walkway in one move, terrified but determined.

I couldn't see a thing – just flickers of movement, where bits of dark seemed a bit less dark – and I could hear raised voices. All I had to do was find the rope and cut it, and they could fight over the limp end of it as long as they liked. Blind in the dark, I moved along the edge of the walkway, feeling for the rope. Then someone jumped on my back, burying their fingers in my hair and wrapping a skinny pair of legs round my waist, and someone else grabbed my legs.

"No, you don't!" said the first,.

"Ain't nobody having our ship but us!" said the second.

The "someones" were small but extremely fired up, so I was knocked down, and the only way to get them off was to roll. Which is what I was doing when the lights went on. One second I was scrabbling in the total dark with who knew what, and the next I was lying in the middle of a pool of the brightest light. On the floor with me were two tiny old blokes, exactly alike, all wrinkles and a great lump of yellowy white hair above each folded face. Standing right next to us were Rivet and Flame, with Bead and Spadey holding up a skinny Supa servant with a bloody leg. And in the middle of it all was Missouri, a stick light strapped to her head with tape, the boat's rope in one arm, and the other arm round the neck of a small red-faced person!

We were all frozen in the white light, all of us amazed for one reason or another. But there wasn't time to say anything because right then a shot sounded over us and a voice yelled,

"Get yer hands up!" The voice and the light came from the tower of the guardhouse above us. Maybe not all the guards were dead. We did as we were told. Missouri and the little white-haired blokes looked fit to explode; Scanner, Rivet, Flame and I all smiled at each other foolishly and put our hands up, as if getting ready to be shot was a big treat.

"We thought you were dead!" whispered Scanner.

"Shuuddup!" came the voice from the tower, followed by another shot over our heads, just to make the point that keeping still and quiet was a good plan.

"Where's Nero?" I breathed out of the corner of my mouth.

Scanner's smile vanished fast.

"Out there," she said, nodding her head towards the open water of the bay, "on the *Uccello*. She's sinking."

There was another shot over us and a voice yelling, "Quiiieeettt!"

I wasn't afraid any more. All that filled my mind was the little craft, on the end of the rope, so close to me. A second of darkness would be enough, and I'd be in it and away. Footsteps ran down from the tower towards us and stopped outside the circle of light. Three armed figures stood looking at us from the shadows. They might have been Supas or Rebels, but either way, we were in danger of being shot. There was a horrible silence. I thought, *If they start shooting, I'll throw myself down and play dead. And when they chuck us in the water, I'll take the boat and I'll find Nero.* I got ready, every muscle hard. Then one of the figures cursed and I felt my body go slack. I knew the voice: it was Bly.

He stepped into the circle of light, with two armed Rebels beside him. He put his hand on my shoulder, and I could feel at once how it trembled. "Sacks," he said softly, "Wichapi!" He looked pleased and frightened at the same time. And I felt bad that I'd run off without telling him why. Then he looked at the tangle of people in front of him, the little white-haired blokes in tatty overalls and the rest in scorched Supas' uniforms. "Who are you?"

Everyone began talking at once. Bly listened for a minute, then made everyone be quiet. "Your craft crashed in the bay?"

"Yes," said Rivet looking at his boots.

"And you men rescued these people, in your boat?"

The two white-heads nodded furiously.

"As you are in Supas' uniforms I can't risk letting you go, I'm afraid. We need to ask you some more questions." Bly turned to his guards. "Take them to the guards' room."

Bly's men bundled everyone towards the steps. The Rebels looked dazed but Scanner managed to speak up. "But we're Rebels! We just blew up the TV tower. One of our men is on our craft in the bay. We need to get him before it sinks…"

"You need to get inside. We'll talk more later."

Scanner tried to speak again, but she was swept up the steps and taken away, with the others.

Bly held me and Missouri by our arms with a grip like iron. When he spoke again, there was flame-bright fierceness in his voice. "Missouri, you know how dangerous this is. Why did you bring my daughter here?"

He looked like he might thump her, but Missouri didn't care. She pulled her arm free and spat on the ground. She looked right at him, with her stuck-out little ledge of bottom lip. "She asked, is why. You didn't listen to her."

He turned to me. "What were you thinking, Sacks? Have you any idea of the risks you have taken coming here? And what were you doing with those people?"

His voice was as hard as stones and as hot as fire, but I was riled up again now thinking of Nero with the water washing over his head. "Didn't you hear what Scanner just told you? There's a boy out there on his craft in the bay, and sinking, and the longer I spend talkin' the less likely it is I'll find him. Now let me go!"

"I can't let you go."

"Not even if he's your son?"

"My son died. Nabisco killed him."

"He didn't. Nero Nabisco is Tadewi. He's been fighting with the Rebels. I know it. I've seen him. I *know* him. I *know* he's my brother. That's why I came here. If only you'd listened to me instead of leaving me behind again!"

Bly wavered. I could see the softness come into his eyes.

"I always told you the boy weren't dead," said Missouri.

"Let *me* go and get him if you won't let her."

Bly looked at Missouri as if he wanted to hit her, then turned to me, not a lot happier. "Why didn't you tell me this before?"

"I was too angry with you… There didn't seem any point." I pulled at his hand. "He's my brother. You have to let me go! *Please, oh please.*" I stopped pulling and waited. I could see he was hesitating.

"No," he stated finally. "No. I can't put tonight's work at risk. I need to find out if their story about the TV tower is true. If it is, I have to find a way of making a broadcast to tell the Workers what's going on. To tell all those who have survived to evacuate the City and make contact with Outsiders. I want you both inside, where you'll be safe, and where you can't get in the way!"

In the half heartbeat as he'd turned from her, Missouri had pulled a gun and shot the light. Suddenly in blackness, I was blind again. I slipped out from Bly's hand and ran down the walkway towards the boat. I couldn't see anything and I tripped on the rope.

"Can't see? Useless you is," said Missouri, and her big hand grabbed my wrist and pulled me into the boat beside her. "I'll show that Bly, getting in the way!" she raged. "Paddle!"

"I'm paddling!"

Missouri had seen the *Uccello* go down and reckoned she knew where to find it, but it was still a big space to search with a

243

stick light and the flashes of fire from burning buildings. The surface of the water stank of leaked fuel – all it would take was a spark and we'd be afloat in a fire-sea. We would never have found him in all that water and dark if it hadn't been for the *Uccello's* last little blink of power. One small green light on her wing cut through the murk and called us to her. She was almost sunk. Just a little of her upturned belly was still above the surface.

Nero was face down on her underside, with water already washing into his mouth and nose. He didn't stir when I called his name, and he was cold, so cold. We got him into the boat and stripped the wet clothes off his body. Next to his skin was my pouch, the only part of him still dry.

"Give him your deer skin," said Missouri. I undid the stiff skin from my body and wrapped it round Nero as best I could. Missouri took off a layer of fur and covered him.

"What can I do, Missouri?"

"Paddle. I'll take you to a place you can do something better."

So we paddled again, one side then the other, one side then the other, towards the sky that was turning a shade of grey and lifting out of the fiery night.

"How d'you know Bly, Missouri?"

"I've known that Bly since long before he was a big secret leader. I was an Outsider and the Supas brought me to the City when they'd killed my people, just like Bly. I served the Nabiscos, as a Worker, same as he did. Mending things was what I did – electrics, communications. I learned all I could about them little wires and sparks that Supas do so much evil with. Reckoned it could come in useful against 'em one day! Bly and me and the others, we worked on the quiet, organizing Rebels and building more Outsider settlements where Supas wouldn't see. When Bly had to run, I stayed, hidden, taking information in and out of the City. Nobody takes much mind of a fat mad woman with raccoon tails on her head! Oh, I've been very useful to that big-shot leader Bly down the years. But he ain't so clever as he thinks he is! He don't know it all. And he don't listen either. No more talk, now. Paddle." And so we did, but with every stroke Missouri was cursing Bly and his "cleverness" under her breath.

Every building along the waterfront was in flames, so the water had begun to look red. In the narrow stretch between one part of the City that burned and the other that didn't, I could see the outline of little rafts with a few people on board, paddling with their hands. But no one was crossing the big empty water of the bay. Perhaps they were frightened that the guard station Bly and his men had taken would still send out boats to catch them.

We paddled on alone, going round little islands of fire burning on the water. Missouri was making for what looked like a tangle of metal sticking up high above the surface. And as we got closer it didn't look any better, though Missouri started to get excited about it. "She's still there, under all that," Missouri said. "The Mother, they called her... *From her beacon hand glows worldwide welcome."* She chanted the words as we drew up to her "Mother". All I could see was rusted metal sheets, bolted and tied in all kinds of ways with no pattern or neatness, to layers and layers of scaffolding and wire. It was a huge thing, as tall as half a Station, and in the dark it seemed almost as long, rusted cold and dirty. A giant metal box. No welcome there, I thought.

Still, Missouri steered the boat to where the thing leaned a little over the water, covering us in shadow. She tied it to a bit of sticking-out pole and then began to feel over the rusty metal surface, chanting softly while she did. "Open up, Mother, lost old Mother. Do you recall what you used to say?

Give me your tired, your poor,
Your huddled masses yearning to breathe free
The wretched refuse of your teeming shore.
Send these, the homeless, tempest-tost to me,
I lift my lamp beside the golden door!"

"That was it, wasn't it? Well tonight you're keepin' your promises!"

There was a click and a creak, and a door opened in the leaning wall above us. Missouri reached in and pulled down a ladder. Together we pulled the slumped weight of Nero up the ladder, onto a narrow little bridge about a man's height above the water. It was a big effort and we sat on the bridge to rest a moment. Missouri shone her light above us. "See!" she said. "There's the Great Mother!"

I looked up into the space and saw a huge golden face above me. The light caught the underside of the chin, the curve of the cheeks, the calm mouth, the blank open eyes. Inside the ugly box was a beautiful giant woman! She leant onto the water, as if she'd got tired of standing up. It lapped around her hips and reached her elbow on one side. On the other side, her arm was raised, or had been once. It had broken just above the shoulder and its end, far above us, was wrapped in layers of plastic.

Missouri spoke softly, talking almost to herself. "You was here before Supas came," she whispered. "You stood tall, with a crown on your head and fire in your hand. You're the Homecoming, you are. You're the Welcome. And now we can use you to talk to the world."

Just when I thought Missouri had forgotten about Nero and me, she scooped him up. As she took him through a dark doorway in the woman's great side, she turned to me, smiling. "Bly ought to remember there's a broadcasting Station in this old lady's head! You wait and see." There was a little room inside, built of old packaging materials and scraps of metal sheeting. The floor sloped badly, but it was dry and, when Missouri lit a candle, perhaps a little welcoming. She scrabbled around in a corner and brought out a bottle and some clean bits of rag. She drank, then handed it to me. "You won't like it," she said, "but take a good pull. 'Twill give you strength. Then use it to clean his cuts. I'm off to get things ready." I heard her footsteps going up stairs above us, until they faded and disappeared.

I took the stopper from the bottle and sipped. It was like liquid blades, but I was hungry and thirsty, and anything in my belly seemed a good thing. I wet a ball of rag with the liquid and cleaned the blood off Nero's face as best I could, then I dipped my finger in the bottle and rubbed the drink round his lips. He licked and started to wake up, enough for me to tip the bottle to his mouth. He coughed, then opened his eyes. He lifted his hand and put it to my face. His cold narrow fingers felt every feature and his eyes filled with tears. "Sacks! You're not dead. You're real. What happened? Where have you been?"

I found my voice had gone, but it didn't seem to matter because Nero was suddenly brimming with words. "Sacks, I found a letter. It was in your pouch, about you and me –" He paused, out of breath. "There's too much to tell you," he went on, "but the most important thing –" He stopped again and took a deep, deep breath. "You are my sister," he finished "and I am your brother."

Nero was right, there was too much to tell, but that was all we needed. I *was* his sister, he *was* my brother; both of us lost, and changed, and found again.

Nero looked around him. "Where are we?"

"Not exactly sure. Inside some giant woman in the bay, below the City."

"The statue! The lady in the bay." He propped himself on an elbow and looked about, more alive every second. "I thought she'd rotted away long ago, wrapped up in all that board and metal. Did you bring me here?"

"Not on my own. There's a woman. Missouri she's called. She's a Rebel..."

"Where is she?"

"Up in the lady's head."

Nero looked confused. There was so much to tell him, and so much I didn't understand. I suddenly felt tired, more tired than I'd ever been in my life. I hadn't imagined finding Nero sick and weak. I hadn't thought further than finding him alive, and ready to run back to the prairie with me. I didn't know what to do with the City falling around us, mad Missouri and her "Great Mother" with a broadcast station where her head should be. I just wanted to curl up there with Nero and sleep until the world had settled, and I had had time to think.

But Missouri's heavy footsteps clattered down the stairs and she burst in, raccoon tails dancing and her high voice alive with excitement, talking as fast as a rocket. "I been up there and checked it all!" she said. "It's all working, I reckon. This here is an old statue. Older than the Supas. They took her over but she's better than they are. Years ago, before TV was in the tower, they had a broadcast station in the Mother's head! Not TV with pictures, just sounds. It went out to every Station, every building, all over the City and all beyond too! There was little boxes everywhere that picked up what they said up there, inside her head."

Nero was sitting very straight now, his eyes beginning to spark, his brain planning so fast that he hadn't stopped to notice Missouri's strangeness. "Radio!" he exclaimed. "It was called radio." Missouri nodded and her tails danced wildly. "My brother found an old box in the Low Tens one time. He said it's what we had before TV – radio. But the Supas gave it up. When I asked Scurro about it, he said it was too easy to do. The boxes were simple to make and they didn't want Workers getting ideas about doing radio themselves."

"It's all still there. I been checking on it all the while, all the years," said Missouri. "Dry and clean. Ready. Ready to use. Tonight. Now. C'mon and see..." She was gone before she finished talking!

I helped Nero to climb the stairs. I explained to him that there were Rebel raids all over the City, that the plan was to destroy it for ever. He began to look really sick again, and started talking as if he were half in a bad dream.

"It went wrong, Sacks. There was too much explosive in the bomb. I never checked it. The whole TV tower went down." He shut his eyes again and sank onto the stairs. "That's what Scurro wanted. He knew about the raids tonight and he wanted to stop the Rebels from taking over the TV tower." His voice was weak and wobbly. "Maybe he's on his way here now to use this place himself..." His fear seemed to give him strength and he began pulling himself up the stairs faster and faster, holding the rails on one side and my arm on the other. "We have to get this to work," he said. "We have to say that Home is a pile of lies, that TV is just to make Workers do what the Supas want, that Outside is safe, that we all have to start again..."

"Bly says we have to warn everyone to get out of the City." I said. I hadn't meant to mention Bly, not yet, but I was fired up with Nero's fear.

"Bly?" Nero stopped dead. "You've met him?"

I nodded. Nero gave a half-smile. "Too much to tell, right?"

I nodded again. Too much to tell and far too much to say the word "father" to each other.

At last we came out into the room that was the radio place. It looked a bit like the *Uccello*'s flight control panel. Missouri shone a torch around. Nero sat down at the top of the stairs, all his energy gone again. "There's no power!" he groaned.

"How much *you* know," snapped Missouri. "There's power – solar panels on the roof and batteries in here." She touched a light switch and a bright, yellowy little bulb in the ceiling came to life! Nero's energy surged up with the power. He got up without the help of my arm. "Yeah! This is fantastic!"

I swear Missouri blushed then. "I been keeping an eye on it all these years," she mumbled. "Just in case!"

"How does it all work?" I asked, but they didn't hear me. Missouri was busy plugging in wires, and Nero was sliding about the floor on a chair with squeaking wheels, his bare legs sticking out of the bottom of my deer skin like he'd never known another way to be. I could have almost laughed out loud!

"Looks like Missouri here knows what she's doing," Nero said. "And I restored a smaller version of this system when I was nine years old!"

There was a clicking sound as he flicked the first switch, but it wasn't the radio machinery coming to life. Nero swung round at the sound. He must have known that click pretty well: Supas' always used the same guns. I'd seen him on TV, so I recognized him. But Scurro Nabisco wasn't looking so smart. His black clothes were ripped and burnt. There was a dark bruise on his pale forehead, and his hands were scratched and smeared with blood. I hoped it was all his own.

"Over here with the weapon, fat girl," he said to Missouri, and she kicked the gun she'd taken from the guard towards him. "On the floor," he told her, "face down, arms above your head." Missouri did as she was told and Scurro's eyes flickered over her then back to me and Nero. He was close enough now for me to hear that his breathing was fast and shallow. It made me think of Mott, lying with the hole in his chest and his life almost gone. But Scurro looked alive, with all the twitchy crackle of a cut cable. "So, Nero," he went on, "you're good with this primitive technology. What with all the time you wasted with rubbish from the Low Tens when you should have been working for your family!"

"You're not my family, Scurro," Nero snarled, Bly's fierceness leaping up in him like a flame. "And what do you know about family loyalty? You trashed your own son."

"Shut up," Scurro had stopped trying to watch over Missouri. His whole attention seemed to be on Nero. He was getting weak! I glanced to where Missouri's gun lay on the floor. Immediately there was a shot and I felt the bullet pass just beside my cheek.

"Switch the system on, Nero, or the next bullet will be *in* her head, not past it." Firing his gun seemed to calm him. His breathing was easier now and his voice less tight. "I'm not here to stop you broadcasting, Nero. I don't *want* to kill your dear sister, as she is so miraculously raised from the grave! No, I want the two of you to make a radio debut together. I want your father to hear your sweet voices from far away, so that he'll come and find you! Now switch it all on, Nero, or I really will have no reason to keep either of you alive!"

Scurro looked wild again, ready to shoot for no reason, but Nero was as calm as ice. "Why don't you switch it on yourself, Scurro?" he said. "Surely you can work out how to use primitive technology like this! No? No. I thought not! You *need* me to do it and *I won't!*"

"I'm warning you, Nero..."

"Warning me of what? Of your intention to kill her? Do

you think that would make me cooperate more willingly? You kill *her* and I don't care what you do to me. You kill *her* and your last chance for revenge is gone, because Bly might not value *his* son any more than you valued *Fortay*! With just me, you won't be able to lure him here!" Nero got up and came towards me, very slowly. He stood between me and Scurro and drew my arms round his waist.

"There, Scurro-sir, I've made it easy for you. Two with one bullet. We are not helping you to kill our father!"

Scurro raised his gun. Shiny white metal it was, with red jewels on the handle, the colour of blood. He looked right down the barrel at Nero, and Nero looked back, without flinching. I tightened my arms round him. "I'm proud of you, Nero."

There was a flicker of movement at the top of the stairs. Scurro's bullet screamed from his gun. For a long moment my heart stopped and the world seemed to fold up inside it. *This is the end of our story*, I thought. *I'll stand here with Nero for ever and ever*. But my heart began to beat again and the world unfolded in a way I didn't expect: we were still alive. It was Scurro who was dead. He lay flat on his face with a thin Rebel blade stuck in his neck. Bly stepped out of the shadow of the staircase and pulled his blade from Scurro's body. Then he helped Missouri to her feet.

"You took your time," she said.

"Well, you always said I was a bit slow, Missouri. You all right?"

"It's just a little hole, is all."

More footsteps clattered on the stairs, and first Scanner then Rivet popped up behind Bly and Missouri, and ran towards us.

"You two all right then?" asked Scanner.

"Reckon you could let Nero go now, Sacks." said Rivet, and I realized I was still hanging on to him.

"Yes. Sorry, Nero." I unclasped my hands from his waist and the four of us stood staring at each other, smiling stupidly, not sure what to do or say.

Then Scanner poked Nero's furry wrapping. "Is that what we all got to wear now?"

"Everybody except you, Scanner. We'd never find a creature with a small enough skin!"

Bead's voice sounded from below.

"Me and Flame got to hold these guards on our own or what?"

"We'd better go," said Rivet.

"Yeah." Scanner nodded. "Don't go running off, right?"

When they were gone, I saw that Missouri had slipped away too, and Bly was left alone with me and Nero. We stood on opposite sides of that strange room, inside the head of the "Great Mother", looking at each other. At last, Bly stepped across the space between us and put out his hands. Nero and I each took one in our own, and held it until it stilled.

onida

EVEN out on the veranda the night had been way too warm for sleeping. But it was nice to be awake so early. To see the strong corn plants reaching for the pale-blue sky, with wisps of mist caught in their broad leaves and tasselled ears, like departing dreams. It would be a good crop again this year! The buffalo meat was drying well too; long, dark strips hung on the wooden frames, on the hottest side of the house. There'd be enough food this winter, even with extra mouths to feed. And there would be extra mouths. Hardly a month passed now without some new arrival. They'd open the door in the morning and there'd be a person curled on the step. Or out in the fields, in the afternoon, someone would shade their eyes and say, "Well, look at that!" and a ragged figure or two would come limping down the broad dirt track.

Onida examined the young ones carefully, questioned them quietly in her deep, soft voice, always wondering whether she would know them, if one day *they* came. It was really light now. There was no point in trying to sleep, thought Onida. She always seemed to be the first up, anyway. But not this morning! William was running towards her from the old Station warehouse, his bandy legs working like pistons. "You gotta come, Onida. Right now. That old radio box is speaking out some good news…"

William had pulled the little box from its place high on the old station wall and placed it, with its wires trailing, in the centre of the table they used for winter dining. Onida sat, leaning her head close to the dusty speaker to hear the faint, crackling broadcast. She listened with a bursting heart, wondering if she was mad to think that from their first words, she knew these voices… The broadcasters were two young Rebels, speaking from an old Supa radio station in Manhattan. They were, they said, inside the head of an ancient statue, a giant woman who had once stood for freedom.

"That's Liberty!" said William. "I remember! She was called the Great Mother when I was a boy!"

"Liberty!" said Creedy. "What a lovely word!"

Almost everyone was gathered round the table now and they all whispered "Liberty" to each other, smiling. Onida shushed them. The young voices had more to say. They alternated between boy and girl; the boy speaking with the flattened tones of a Supa, the girl with the lilt of a Worker. They were young to be reporting on such momentous events.

"...raids have taken place across the greatest of the remaining Supa cities, hitting major targets and all Supa buildings. Rebel activities are being coordinated by the legendary Outsider Chieftain, Winema Bly..."

Onida put both of her big hands flat on the table so that she wouldn't fall through it. She concentrated on breathing slowly and listening hard:

"...all of Manhattan is in flames. Rebels and Outsiders are helping Workers evacuate the City. All Workers should leave Manhattan across the Sound between Spires 36 and 37. All Outsider settlements should be ready to accept refugees. Everyone should listen for the next broadcast at the same time tomorrow..."

The broadcast was about to end! Onida's ability to stay calm was deserting her. She felt she might just sit at the table and wait for twenty-four hours without moving until she could hear those voices again. She wanted to go on hearing them. She wanted some final clue, some last word that would seal her joy and let it free. It came at last:

"This is Sacks Wichapi..." said the girl.

"...and Nero Tadewi..." said the boy.

"...signing off from Liberty Radio," they said together, "on Planet Earth, our Home, where we all belong."

Wichapi, Tadewi, Bly... The names sung inside Onida like another heartbeat. While everyone hugged and danced around the table in excitement, she quietly went out into the corn.

She felt the soil under her feet and the sun on her skin; she breathed deeply and felt all the good Earth grow sweeter to her, now she knew – knew for sure – that she still shared it with her family.

Twelve-year-old MapHead is a visitor from a world that exists side by side with our own. The young traveller has come to meet his mortal mother for the first time. But, for all his dazzling alien powers, can MapHead master the language of the human heart?

Two award-winning novels now available in one volume.

"Weird and wonderful. It's like nothing you'll ever have read before." *Young Telegraph*

"Strange, poetic, funny, unforgettable." *The Guardian*

Winner of the Guardian Fiction Prize and Highly Commended for the Carnegie Medal

BY LESLEY HOWARTH

"We went to the moon to have fun, but the moon turned out to completely suck."

Titus doesn't think much of the moon. But then Titus doesn't think much period. He's got his "feed" – an Internet implant linked directly into his brain – to do his thinking for him.

But then Titus meets Violet, a girl who cares what's happening to the world, and challenges everything Titus and his friends hold dear. A girl who decides to fight the feed...

"An extraordinary, intelligent state-of-the-Western-world satire set in an imagined future... A treat for jaded palates... Everyone should read it." *The Bookseller*

BY M. T. ANDERSON

When his guardian dies in suspicious circumstances, fourteen-year-old Alex Rider finds his world turned upside down.

Within days he's gone from schoolboy to superspy. Forcibly recruited into MI6, Alex has to take part in gruelling SAS training exercises; then, armed with his own special set of secret gadgets, he's off on his first mission. But Alex soon finds himself in mortal danger. It looks as if his first assignment may well be his last...

"Horowitz will grip you with suspense, daring and cheek – and that's just the first page! ... Prepare for action scenes as fast as a movie." *The Times*

First in the explosive Alex Rider series!

BY ANTHONY HOROWITZ

In a newspaper office, Paul Faustino, South America's top football writer, sits opposite the man they call El Gato – the Cat – the world's greatest goalkeeper. On the table between them stands the World Cup...

In the hours that follow, El Gato tells his incredible life story – how he, a poor logger's son, learns to become a World Cup-winning goalkeeper so good he is almost unbeatable. And the most remarkable part of this story is the man who teaches him – the mysterious Keeper, who haunts a football pitch at the heart of the claustrophobic forest.

This extraordinary gripping tale pulses with the rhythms of football and the rainforest.

BY MAL PEET

"Don't cry. We won't be parted, I promise."

It is 1662 and England is reeling from the after-effects of civil war, with its clashes of faith and culture. Seventeen-year-old Will returns home after completing his studies, to begin an apprenticeship arranged by his wealthy father. Susanna, a young Quaker girl, leaves her family to become a servant in the same town.

Theirs is a story that speaks across the centuries, telling of love and the struggle to stay true to what is most important – despite parents, society and even the law.

But is the love between Will and Susanna strong enough to survive – no matter what?

BY ANN TURNBULL